"There's nothing [barcode] ***with wanting me***

Tag said coaxingly.

"I'm afraid," Julie murmured.

His hand slid down to her throat, fingers spreading wide over the soft skin. "Of what?"

"Falling in love with you." Her eyes widened as she realized what she had let slip. She stepped back from him. "Oh, no. I didn't—" But there was no way to deny what she had said.

Tag was watching her, his eyes narrowed and intent. "Would that be so horrible? To love me?"

"No. Not at all." Feeling flooded her chest at the thought of loving Tag. "It would be wonderful."

His face changed subtly, became softer and warmer.

"The problem is afterwards, when you leave."

Dear Reader,

I have several very exciting things to talk about this month; in fact, it's hard to know where to begin. How about with a piece of news some of you have been waiting years to hear?

In 1986, Kristin James wrote a novel for Silhouette Intimate Moments called *A Very Special Favor.* The hero of that book had two brothers, and over the years, I've received quite a lot of letters asking for their stories. This month, I'm glad to oblige with *Salt of the Earth,* the first step in completing THE MARSHALLS, a family-based trilogy. In August look for *The Letter of the Law,* to complete the series. And here's another piece of terrific news: anyone who missed *A Very Special Favor* the first time around will get a second chance to purchase it this fall, as part of a special in-store promotion. Look for it in your bookstores.

If that's not enough excitement for you, here's more: Kay Hooper is back with *The Haviland Touch,* a sequel to her first—and very popular—Intimate Moments novel, *Enemy Mine.* Of course, this suspenseful and adventure-filled story stands on its own, so whether you've read that first book or not, you have a treat in store this month.

Round out the month with Heather Graham Pozzessere's *Snowfire,* a nice wintry story to balance the summer heat, and Marilyn Tracy's *Echoes of the Garden,* in which long-estranged lovers are brought together by their love for their son. In coming months, look for books by Nora Roberts, Linda Howard, Kathleen Eagle, Naomi Horton, Emilie Richards and all of the other wonderful authors who make Silhouette Intimate Moments one of the most exciting series in romance fiction today.

Leslie Wainger
Senior Editor and
Editorial Coordinator

KRISTIN JAMES

Salt of the Earth

SILHOUETTE·INTIMATE·MOMENTS®

Published by Silhouette Books New York

America's Publisher of Contemporary Romance

SILHOUETTE BOOKS
300 East 42nd St., New York, N.Y. 10017

SALT OF THE EARTH

Copyright © 1991 by Candace Camp

ISBN: 0-373-07385-2

First Silhouette Books printing June 1991

Printed in the U.S.A.

Books by Kristin James

Silhouette Intimate Moments

Dreams of Evening #1
The Amber Sky #17
Morning Star #45
Secret Fires #69
Worlds Apart #89
Cutter's Lady #125
*A Very Special Favor #136
*Salt of the Earth #385

*The Marshalls

KRISTIN JAMES,

a former attorney, is married to a family counselor, and they have a young daughter. Her family and her writing keep her busy, but when she does have free time, she loves to read. In addition to her contemporary romances, she has written several historicals.

To the Cliftons, Richard, Sharon, Melinda and
Catherine, for their many contributions to this book

Chapter 1

Adam Marshall frowned down at the open file folder, oblivious to the bustle and noise of the restaurant around him. Tag was late, as usual, and Adam was taking advantage of the time to slip in some work.

"That bad, huh?" The masculine voice was light and teasing.

Adam recognized it immediately and looked up, smiling. "Hello, Tag."

"Hi." Tag was dressed in a casual shirt and slacks, unlike his older brother, who wore the attorneys' uniform of a three-piece suit. Even so, Tag managed to look as if he'd just stepped out of the pages of a magazine or off a movie set.

The two brothers resembled each other, both being tall and slender with inky black hair and blue eyes. Adam, the elder of the pair, was considered handsome, but Tag's clear-cut features bordered on perfection. From the time Tag was sixteen, wherever he went female heads turned. By now, everyone in the family had gotten used to it.

Tag sat down, shaking his head in bemusement. "Do you and James ever sit down and enjoy a meal in peace? Without a legal file in front of you?"

Adam gave him a rueful smile and closed the folder, then set it back in his briefcase. "On occasion."

"It's a good thing you've got an adoring wife."

"Yeah. Isn't it?" Adam's smile broadened. He had been married a year now, and he and Emily were still passionately in love. "Emily's a jewel."

Tag flipped open the menu and began to study it.

"How are things going?" Adam asked.

Tag flashed him a disgusted look. "Don't ask."

"Oh. I see."

Tag sighed and snapped the menu shut. "Dad and I had a fight again last night."

"What about?"

"Holly Bangston."

"Harold Bangston's daughter?"

"The same. I've been going out with her some the last few months. Nothing serious. We're just friends. She's a nice girl, and we get along well, but that's it. She knows it. I know it. But our father decided that it would be a wonderful idea for me to marry her."

Adam raised an eyebrow. "Leith Marshall is into matchmaking now?"

"He's into wanting me to settle down and become a responsible citizen."

"Ah."

"Shades of law school. And the bank. And every other thing he's wanted me to do. He wants me to 'act like a Marshall.'"

Adam sighed. His father had never been able to handle Taggart. Leith Marshall could not understand why his youngest son was so different. Why he didn't want to be an attorney like three-fourths of the Marshall clan was, or at least a banker, like the other quarter. When Tag was younger their father had pushed him into law school. Tag had dropped out after a year. He found law deadly dull, and the thought of being cooped up in some office, mounds of files and books stacked up all around him, was suffocating to him. He had also tried a job in one of his uncle's banks, with even less spectacular results. Luckily he'd been wise enough to turn down the Taggart uncles' offer to let him join the management team at Taggart Mills.

Leith had been astounded—and enraged. He could not understand how one of his sons could have turned out to be so lazy and irresponsible. The Marshalls had always prided themselves on being not only wealthy and well-bred, but also hardworking, productive citizens.

Adam had tried on several occasions to explain to his father that Tag was not lazy and irresponsible. He was simply different. He was a good, kindhearted man, and he was both willing to and capable of working hard whenever he had to. Adam had seen him working on his sailboat too often not to realize how hard he could work. It was simply that Tag did not have the same kind of driven, competitive spirit that James, Adam and their father did. He didn't have any interest in law or banking or any other occupation that cooped him up inside. Tag loved the outdoors. He enjoyed riding and sailing, and in such areas he excelled. But Adam had never been able to make Leith understand. To Leith, Tag remained a failure.

"You see," Tag went on, "Dad knows Harold Bangston, and he thinks it would be grand to have me marry a tobacco heir's daughter. She is, after all, from 'a very good family.'" Tag mimicked his father's aristocratic tones so well that Adam had to chuckle.

"When I told him that I had no plans to marry Holly he had a fit. He said that he had thought I was showing signs of growing up, that he had hoped I was about to marry and settle down and maybe even do something constructive with my life. I told him that I wasn't about to marry someone I didn't love just to satisfy his need for me to be respectable." Tag grimaced and made a dismissive gesture with his hand. "Well, so it went. You've heard a few of our arguments."

Adam nodded. "Unfortunately."

Tag and his father didn't seem capable of being around each other without fighting; they'd been doing it since Tag was a boy. It had been best for all concerned when Tag had inherited a substantial trust fund at the age of twenty-three and moved out.

"Anyway, finally it ended with him throwing down his napkin and jumping up from the table to tell me that I would doubtless never get married because I was incapable of loving anyone but myself."

Adam frowned. "You know he didn't mean that. He gets so bent out of shape sometimes that he speaks without thinking."

Tag shrugged. "No. I think he really believes it. At times I've wondered about it myself. I mean, I'm thirty years old, and I've never found a woman I could stand for longer than a couple of months." He shot a teasing grin at his brother. "Too bad you married Emily. You took the best woman in town off the market."

"You'll find someone. Give yourself time. You're only thirty."

"Yeah. But when do you think I'm going to figure out what I want to be when I grow up?"

Adam smiled. "I don't know."

The waiter appeared at their table, looking harried; the restaurant was always very busy at noon on weekdays. He scribbled their order down on his pad and scurried off. Adam looked at his brother thoughtfully. There was something wrong with Tag's tone.

"It's more than the argument with Dad, isn't it? You're upset about something else."

Tag grimaced. "I don't know. Sometimes I wonder if Dad is right. Maybe I am a lazy, irresponsible bum. The past few weeks—well, I've been bored and tired and disgusted with myself. I feel like I'm drifting."

"Drifting?"

"Yeah. Without purpose. Everything I do seems stale and boring. I'm tired of seeing the same people and chatting about the same things at parties and dances and receptions that differ only in the particulars. It doesn't matter where I go—a cocktail party, a charity ball, or even tennis and lunch at the Club. It all boils down to the same thing. Everyone is there to see and be seen, and the conversation is centered around themselves, their friends—and enemies—and the general state of Society, with a capital *S,* as it exists in Winston-Salem, North Carolina, today."

"Now you sound like James." James, the middle brother, was the most serious of the three. Instead of joining his father's law firm as Adam had, he had become a federal prosecuting attorney. He was usually involved in some cause or another, and he was often sarcastically derisive about the social set to which the Marshalls belonged.

"God forbid," Tag quipped, rolling his eyes. He loved James, but they didn't get along as he and Adam did. James thought Tag was a frivolous person, a lightweight, and he often took what he felt was an older brother's prerogative to lecture Tag.

"Oh, come on, James isn't that bad. He has your best interests at heart."

"I'm sure he does. And it's undoubtedly frustrating for him that he can't organize me into a clone of himself."

Adam had to smile. "No doubt." He paused. "'So you're bored right now. Why not do something? Sail up the Intercoastal Waterway."

"I've done it. Twice. I can't even get interested in sailing nowadays. I've hardly had the boat out twice this summer. I still go riding, but that can take up only so much of my time." Tag sighed. "I feel restless. Useless. Carey Jamison asked me to go to Florida with him, but I didn't want to. This gorgeous woman from New York who I met in St. Kitts last year wants me to join her there again this year, and I turned her down. Am I going crazy? I never felt like this before."

Adam shrugged. "I doubt you're going crazy. Maybe you simply need to commit to something—or someone."

"Is that another way of saying I should get a job or get married?"

Adam smiled. "No. I didn't mean it that way. But everyone needs something to hold on to or else you *are* drifting through life."

"Yeah, but what should *I* hold on to? That's the problem." Tag sighed. "Lately I've wished I could just get away."

"Why don't you? Go down to the house at Hilton Head."

Tag shook his head. "No. I want to get farther away than that. I'm tired of the whole Eastern Seaboard. Of this life-style. Of being a Marshall and a Taggart."

Adam thought for a moment, his forefinger rubbing his upper lip in a habitual gesture of concentration. Suddenly he stopped and pointed to Tag. "I've got it. How about that ranch Dad bought as a tax write-off? The one in Texas. Drinkwater or someplace. I'm certain there's a house there that's unused."

Tag's forehead creased as he considered it. "It's certainly different. And it is far away from here. Far away from my life-style, too.

"No society gatherings," Adam said smiling.

"You know, the more I think about it, the more I like it." He would be unknown, anonymous. There would be no expectations of how he should or shouldn't act. No tangle of social obligations, no well-meaning friends to suck him into going to this party or that play. He could think. He could be alone. And maybe he would find an answer to the aimlessness that afflicted him.

Tag grinned and raised his water glass in a salute. "Thanks, Adam. I think I'll do it. Here's to Backwater, Texas."

"Drinkwater," Adam corrected laughingly. "No, I don't think that's quite it, either. Maybe it's Drinkman."

"Drinkman. Drinkmeyer. Whatever it is, maybe it'll be the solution to my problems."

"Hear, hear."

"I think I'll leave tomorrow."

Julie was awakened by the touch of hot, moist breath against her ear. A cold nose nuzzled her neck. It was accompanied by the rhythmic sound of a large tail thumping against her bedside stand.

"Jackson, you're better than an alarm clock," she groaned, shoving the dog's big head away and rolling over onto her back. There was a loud snuffle and a whine, and Julie opened one eye and looked at her dog. Part collie, part Australian shepherd and many parts unknown, he was black and white and stood with his head on a level with her bed. At the moment he was waiting expectantly, his mouth open, tongue lolling out of an idiotic grin.

Julie made an exasperated noise and pushed the bed covers aside. Jackson backed up, his entire rear end wiggling with the enthusiasm of his tail wags. Julie stumbled blearily out of the bedroom and down the stairs to open the front door. Jackson followed, his movements a little slow on the stairs; he was thirteen years old and inclined to arthritis first thing in the morning.

By the time Julie opened the screen door leading onto the front porch, Jackson had acquired his usual morning entourage of the poodle and the dachshund, and they all burst out onto the porch together. In a rush the two hunting dogs and the part-Irish setter came bounding around the side of the house to join them, barking with early-morning high spirits, and then the entire pack went tearing off down the dirt driveway. No matter how old Jackson might be getting, Julie thought, it never seemed to stop him from running after anything that moved.

She drew a deep breath and moved to the railing that ran around the old farmhouse porch. It was a beautiful September morning, with a hint of coolness in the air. The sun had lightened the sky and tinted the trees with gold but hadn't risen over the treetops yet. There were wisps of fog here and there, and in the distance she could see a blanket of fog hanging over the pond.

She perched on the railing and leaned back against one of the slender columns. She had seen the view thousands of times, yet somehow, in the golden wash of morning, it looked beautiful and new all over again. Julie breathed in the clean, faintly grass-scented air and closed her eyes, reveling in the moment of serenity.

It didn't last long. Feet pounded down the stairs inside and a moment later the kitchen radio came on, blasting out a country song.

Julie sighed and stood up. It was time to get back to the real world. She slid off the railing and went inside, then walked down the hall and stuck her head into the kitchen. Cathy was at the counter singing along with the radio and pouring cereal into a bowl.

"Hey. How you doing?"

Her younger sister swung around. At fifteen Cathy was already taller than Julie, but her figure was still straight as a stick and absurdly thin. She was dressed in her usual uniform of jeans and a T-shirt, and even though the weather was too warm for it, she proudly wore her new blue Future Farmers of America jacket over the T-shirt.

"Hi, Julie." Cathy poured milk over the large pile of cereal and shoveled a spoonful into her mouth. "Can you take me to school this morning?"

"Why can't you go with Riley?"

Cathy grimaced. "He's always late—you know that. I gotta get there early this morning. FFA meeting."

"Okay. But you'll have to hustle to get the animals fed by the time I leave."

"Sure thing." Cathy took another spoonful and went out the door onto the small porch to pull on her muddy work boots.

Julie grabbed a piece of raisin bread and went upstairs. At the top of the stairs she paused and glanced into Riley and Lyle's bedroom. The radio was playing loudly, tuned to a rock station out of Austin, and it created a discordant din of noise when coupled with the country and western station Cathy had left on in her own room down the hall. On the far side of the boys' room a large lump in one twin bed indicated that Lyle was there with the covers pulled up over his head, somehow managing to sleep through the noise of Riley's radio. Riley—the biggest sleepyhead of the family—was up and had managed to start dressing, but he had gotten sidetracked somewhere along the way and was now sitting sideways in a chair, jeans on but shirtless, with a spiral notebook and pen in his hand, alternately writing and drumming with the pen in time with the music.

"Better get moving, Riley."

He swung his head around and smiled. "Sure, Julie." At seventeen he was all arms and legs, though his chest was beginning to fill out. His dark brown hair was too long and shaggy as far as Julie was concerned, and he was exasperatingly slow and dreamy, but he was still the same sweet boy he had always been, with a smile that would warm the coldest heart.

Julie could tell by the vague look in her brother's brown eyes that he was lost in some far-off world, and she would be lucky if he had moved an inch from that chair by the time she had finished getting ready. She shook her head, smiling to herself as she went down the hall and into the bathroom. There were only two bathrooms in their large, old-fashioned house, and it was often a struggle for five adults and near-adults to get ready in the morning. Of course, it had been even worse a few years back, before Jill got married. Jilly had been a real bathroom hog.

It helped that Lyle, commuting back and forth to a nearby junior college, had an evening job at a restaurant and had arranged his classes to start late, so at least he was out of the morning competition. And Granddad apparently hadn't come in last night at all. So for once Julie had the bathroom to herself without the threat of interference. But she didn't have time to enjoy the luxury; there were too many things to do at the store before it opened, and she still had to make sure Cathy got to school early.

She showered and dressed, then pulled back her thick red-brown hair into the single braid in which she usually wore it. She slapped on a little makeup and was through with her morning toilette. Julie didn't have time to waste on trying to look good, and, fortunately, she didn't really need much. Like most of the Farrell family she was tall and had a lithe, attractive figure, kept that way by the physically active life she led.

Her long legs and slender figure looked good in the blue jeans that were her standard form of dress. She

had a strong, vivid face, with high, prominent cheek-
bones, a determined chin, and straight slashes of eyebrows above large gray-green eyes. Her eyes tilted up
a little at the outside corners, giving her face an almost exotic attractiveness. Not quite beautiful, but
definitely compelling. It might have been too strong a
face had it not been for the lovely translucent quality
of her skin, which added a certain softness to her
looks.

Julie peeked into Riley's room again on her way
downstairs and was pleased to see that at least he'd
managed to make it out of the room. She heard him
in the kitchen fixing his breakfast and she called out
"goodbye" as she grabbed her purse and keys off the
hall table and headed out the front door.

She stopped on the front porch and grimaced as she
realized that since Granddad had taken the new
pickup, she would have to take the old one. "New"
was a relative term, for their big 1979 model pickup
truck was new only in relation to the 1960s contrap-
tion presently sitting beside the house. Cathy, coming
up from the barn, groaned loudly when she saw Julie
heading toward it.

"Do we have to take that?"

Julie shot her a look. "Unless you'd rather wait for
your brother."

"No. I'm coming. Just let me wash my hands."

"You've got plenty of time." It always took several
minutes to get the old truck started and warmed up,
even in good weather.

"I know." Cathy's voice was filled with disgust.

The pickup was black, though several scratches and
peeling areas revealed varying colors beneath that. It
was battered, and the tailgate was so badly dented that

it no longer closed and was wired shut with baling wire. Some whimsical former owner had added a grillwork gate, spray-painted a bright silver, directly behind the cab. Cathy always said sneeringly that it looked more like a bedstead than anything else. Its steering and breaks were definitely manual, and its many-times-rebuilt transmission had a hard time moving into any gear. The best thing that could be said about it was that it ran—given some coddling—and could be used in a pinch. But it had been their father's "tinkering vehicle," on which he had spent many hours working, and Julie couldn't bring herself to get rid of it. Even Cathy, who found riding in it acutely embarrassing, never suggested selling it to the junkyard.

Besides, at times like this, when their car was on the blink and Julie couldn't spare the five hundred dollars it would take to get it repaired, the old pickup came in handy. Still, there were moments—such as when Julie saw some sporty little car pass her on the highway—when she thought longingly of selling the old wreck and buying something else. But then she would remind herself that a sports car would be of no practical use to her family, and that the pickup wouldn't bring in enough to make it worth selling, anyway. Julie was normal enough to want the things that any other twenty-five-year-old woman wanted, but she was too responsible to pursue them.

She was always very much aware of the reason why she was so different; she'd had a family to take care of since she was nineteen. She had had to grow up fast when her parents were killed in a car crash six years earlier. There had been no one else to watch over the other Farrell children, all of whom had been under

eighteen years of age, except Julie. While Granddad
had been able to get legal custody, something the court
was reluctant to give to a nineteen-year-old, Julie had
known that he couldn't take care of them without her.
Their grandfather was getting a little old to be able to
handle four lively children, no matter how good his
health was. Besides, charming as Horace Farrell was,
he was not the sort to provide a constant, stable family life. He didn't like to be chained to schedules or
weighed down by the mundane things in life, such as
dinner times or baseball practices or conferences with
teachers. So Julie had taken on the burden, without
complaint and without regret. Granddad had told her
she had a lot of "grit," but she knew it wasn't that. It
was simply love for her family. There was no way that
she would leave her brothers and sisters to fend for
themselves, just as there was no way that she would
betray her beloved parents' trust in her.

Julie climbed up into the cab and slipped the key in,
then put in the clutch and pumped the gas, turning the
key in precisely the way it took to get the cranky old
truck going. It took five tries before the truck finally
shuddered to life, and even then it quit before it really
got going. Cathy had gotten back from the house,
hands washed and holding her schoolbooks, by the
time it started for good.

Julie revved the engine, and black smoke belched
out of the tailpipe. She let the truck warm up at full
throttle for a few minutes, then put it into gear, and
the old truck lurched out of the side yard and onto the
dirt driveway that led to the highway. The driveway
itself was short, which was fortunate, since it was also
deeply rutted. Cathy automatically braced herself with
one hand against the ceiling; with the other hand she

held on tightly to her books. Julie clung to the steering wheel as they bounced and squeaked and jolted their way down to the highway. Both of them were too accustomed to the rough ride to even notice it much anymore.

Once on the highway Julie opened it up—the truck was old, but it could still move—and they reached the school complex in ten minutes. Julie let Cathy out by the high school, then continued down the highway to the center of town. At the corner of Main she turned right and drove past the little cluster of buildings that passed for downtown in Brinkman, Texas. The streets were empty. Workers and employers were only beginning to arrive and open up their businesses. As she passed, anyone who was on the sidewalk turned to wave at her. In a town the size of Brinkman, not only did everyone know you, they knew your car, as well, and often even your routine.

Julie didn't mind. That was part of life in a small town, and she loved it. There was a sense of community here—a closeness, almost like a large, loosely connected family. And if there were people she didn't like and times when the interest everyone took in everyone else's affairs was distinctly annoying, well, families could be just as annoying and sometimes included people you didn't like, too. She belonged here; she was a part of it. She had lived in Brinkman all her life, except for the year she spent at college before her parents' death, and she expected to live out the rest of her life here, as well. It wasn't that she didn't want to see other places or travel; if she ever had the time or the money she would. But she would always come back, sooner or later. Her roots went deep into this land and this town. The Farrells and McCutcheons had settled here not long after the Civil War, and there had been Farrells and McCutcheons living here ever since. They were part of Brinkman, and Brinkman was a part of them.

Two blocks past the bank lay Farrell's Feed and Seed store. Julie pulled into the wide dirt parking area beside it and stopped off to the right, where the truck would not get in the way of people driving to the dock to load sacks of feed. She unlocked the side door to the store and went inside, where she went about her usual morning tasks of sweeping, making coffee and preparing the bank deposit of receipts from the night before.

At eight-thirty she unlocked the front door and turned over the Closed sign to read Open. Then she poured a cup of coffee and sat down on the high stool behind the counter to organize the cash register receipts for August to take to their accountant. She had finished that task, as well as waited on her first customer of the day, when Granddad came strolling in through the side door.

"Hello, darlin'," he greeted her cheerfully and planted a kiss on her forehead. "Sorry I overslept."

"No doubt you had a tiring night," Julie said dryly.

He chuckled. "Now, you wouldn't begrudge an old man his few simple pleasures, would you?"

Julie gave an indelicate snort. "Old" and "simple pleasures" were not words one would think of in connection with Horace Farrell. Almost seventy, her grandfather was still wiry and strong, and he wore his Western clothes and wide-brimmed hat with flair. His hair was snow white but full and slightly wavy, and his brown eyes always had a mischievous twinkle in them. He wasn't a typical grandfather by any means—more inclined to go out honky-tonking than to sit on the front porch rocking—but he couldn't have been more loving with or received more love from his grandchildren. He and Julie often teased each other, but underneath their playful manner lay a solid bedrock of affection.

"You know, Granddad, there are those who'd say you're getting a mite old for that sort of thing."

He grinned, shaking his head. "Never to old to go out with a good-looking woman."

"But think of the effect your spending the whole night with Riette could have on Riley's and Cathy's young minds."

Horace let out a hoot of laughter. "If those two haven't figured it out by now..."

Julie tried unsuccessfully to smother her giggle. "Granddad, you're incorrigible. If they grow up to be sex fiends we'll know who to blame."

"Yeah," he retorted. "Their starchy sister."

Julie waggled her forefinger at him. "You're going to pay for that one."

The bell over the front door tinkled, and they turned to see who had entered. It was Mike Kubiak, the manager of the B & K Cattle Company, the biggest cattle operation in the area and also the store's largest account.

"Hi, Mike," Horace greeted him cheerfully. "Want a cup of coffee?"

"Yeah, that'd be real nice." Mike was a soft-spoken man. Julie always thought of him as the very picture of the quiet, slow-talking Texas cowboy in Westerns. He wasn't tall, but he was well-built, with a powerful chest and arms that came from years of hard physical labor, not daily workouts with a machine. He wore

jeans and boots, as most of the men around Brinkman did, and his felt cowboy hat was stained and
crumpled from years of wear in the sun, rain and
wind. His hair was sandy, his eyes a light blue, and his
skin would have been fair, too, if he hadn't spent so
much time in the sun that it had turned a perpetual
reddish tan.

Mike took a cup of coffee from Horace and leaned
against the counter. Julie was aware that he wanted to
talk to her. It had been obvious for some time now
that he was interested in her. He had been three years
ahead of her in school and had dated one of the
cheerleaders. He and the cheerleader had gotten married halfway through college, but it hadn't worked
out, and he had been divorced for three years. For the
past year he had been trying in his slow, rather shy way
to work up a romance with Julie. That knowledge—
and the fact that she didn't want to date him—made
her unusually tongue-tied whenever he was around.

Fortunately, Horace was never tongue-tied.
"How're things going out at your place?"

"Fine. No problems. We'll be vaccinating the calves
in a few weeks. We could use Riley's help." Riley often
worked part-time at the B & K, helping out during
peak times. It was generally hard work, but good
money for him.

"Sure. Just name the day."

"How's Benny?" Horace asked. Benny was Mike's
uncle, who had been manager of the cattle company
before him. Mike was on the young side to hold the
position, but he had worked on the ranch almost his
whole life, and he had been a natural to take over
when his uncle had had a heart attack two years before.

"Fine. He's enjoying retirement."

There was silence for a moment. Mike shifted from one foot to the other and studied the cup of coffee in his hands. "We got one of the owners coming to visit," he said finally, relieved to have come up with a topic of conversation.

"Oh, really?" Julie asked, mildly interested. The ranch hadn't been owned by anyone local since before she could remember. For most of her life it had been owned by a Houston oilman who had kept it more or less as a hobby, a showplace for his prize registered cattle. But several years ago, after the oil business crashed, the man had had to sell it. It had gone through two or three different owners since then, the most recent of which was a group in North Carolina.

"Yeah. Well, not really the owner, but the son of the owner—or maybe it's the grandson."

"Why's he coming?"

"I'm not sure. It sounded like he was in trouble with the old man or something and Mr. Marshall was kicking him out, sending him out here to cool his heels for a while."

"Exiled to Brinkman." Julie chuckled.

"I guess. I got the impression he was sorta the black sheep of the family. I gotta go pick him up at the airport in Austin this afternoon." He made a face.

Julie knew Mike didn't relish the idea of babysitting some wild and pampered rich man's son. "How long's he going to stay?"

"Who knows? Till he straightens up, I imagine. I just hope I don't have to look after him all the time. You know he'll be bored in two days."

"Or less."

Once the conversation got rolling, Horace went through the back door into the barnlike area where the sacks of feed were stored. Julie was sure he had nothing to do back there; he just wanted to leave her alone with Mike. Irritatingly, he had begun to matchmake between the two of them lately.

With the story of the wayward Marshall son over, Julie and Mike fell into silence again. Mike took a final sip of his coffee and set it down on the counter. Julie decided to take that as a sign that the idle chatting was over and he was ready to do business. She slid off her stool and said cheerfully, "Well, what can we do for you today?"

"I just dropped in to get the minerals. I want a ton of Eight-Eight."

"I'm sorry. Our shipment hasn't arrived yet."

He looked surprised. "I thought it always came on Tuesday."

"It does. But it's been delayed. I called yesterday afternoon when it hadn't arrived, and they said they'd get it here this morning."

"Oh. Okay. Well, I have to run up to Austin pretty soon and pick up this Marshall guy. Why don't I drop by on the way back from the airport this afternoon?"

"Great. It should be here by then." She would be pulling out her hair if it weren't. This was not the first time she'd had shipping problems with this feed company, one of two from which they purchased their inventory. If it weren't for the fact that they carried a better quality of feed, she would simply drop them.

He nodded. "I need a few range cubes, too. I'll pick 'em up at the same time. Five sacks."

"Okay. We'll have everything ready to be loaded."

Mike turned as though to walk away, then swung back. "I was wondering...about the game Friday night...if maybe I could take you to it."

"I'm sorry. I already made plans to go with Vicky Kowalski."

"Oh. Sure. Well, maybe another time."

"Yeah. Say—why don't you meet us there? We could all sit together." She grinned. "You could even bring your prodigal son. That'd give him a real taste of small town life."

His face brightened. "Okay. That sounds good. I don't know about the Marshall guy, though. I'll probably be trying to avoid him by that time."

Julie smiled. Mike walked out the front door, and Julie called goodbye. A second later Horace came back in from the back room.

Julie turned and shot him a glare. "Just what did you think you were doing?"

"Why, being discreet and obliging, what else?" Her grandfather put on a look of supreme innocence.

"Don't give me that. You know there's nothing going on between Mike and me. You're just trying to work something up!"

"The boy's such a slow starter, it looked to me like he needed a little help. If I left it up to him, it'd probably be Christmas before he asked you out."

"So? I certainly wouldn't mind. Why do you want to put me in such an awkward position? He's one of our best customers, not just for the Cattle Company, but for the cattle he runs on his own place, too. I can't be rude to him."

"Then don't be. Go out with him."

"I don't want to go out with him."

"Well, why in blue blazes not? He's a nice-looking boy, has a good job, and he's smart enough. What you got against him?"

"I don't have anything against him. I like Mike. Just not in that way."

"Hell's bells, girl, I'm not asking you to marry him! Just go out with him and have some fun!"

"Oh, Granddad, that'd be fine if you were talking about someone else. I went out with Buddy Carroll like that last year. But Mike's not the kind of guy you can date casually. He's too serious. Too slow. Once he starts dating you, he sticks with it. I'd lay odds on it. Before you knew it, he'd be talking about getting engaged. Then I'd feel like a real heel breaking up with him."

"Maybe. But you might have fallen for him by then, too. Did you ever think of that?"

"I don't think it's likely. Besides, Vicky is crazy about him." And she was quite pleased with herself for having arranged for Mike to be thrown together with Vicky Kowalski Friday night. Julie was sure she could find an easy way to detach herself from the threesome. "I couldn't do that to her."

"Vicky Kowalski." He made a dismissive gesture. "Let Vicky look out for herself. She's a pretty girl— she won't have any trouble finding another boy."

"Meaning *I* would?" Julie asked indignantly, setting her hands on her hips.

He rolled his eyes. "Meaning Vicky would make the effort. *You* wouldn't."

"Oh, Grampy," she said, reverting to her childhood name for him. She went around the counter and gave him a hug. "You worry too much about me."

"And who else would if I didn't?" He squeezed her tightly. "You're everybody else's mother hen. But you've got nobody to fuss over you."

"You're the best," she whispered. "How could I ever fall in love with a man when I've got you to compare him to?" She was only partly teasing when she said it. Her family was her life. There was little room in it for outsiders.

Her grandfather snorted in disbelief, but he hugged her hard to him for an instant.

It wasn't a very busy day. The delivery from the feed mill came later in the morning and was unloaded, and they had enough spare time to set aside the B & K order close to the loading dock for Mike to pick up when he came by.

A little before closing time Julie saw Mike's pickup pull into the lot. He drove straight around to the loading dock, and she and Horace went to help him load the sacks.

"Sorry I didn't make it earlier," Mike apologized as they walked toward him. His face was stamped with irritation. "The plane was an hour late."

"That's okay." Julie and her grandfather picked up a large sack together and carried it to the truck bed, then tossed it in. Julie peered curiously through the back window of the cab, hoping to get a glimpse of the wastrel son Mike had been talking about earlier that morning, but all she could see was the back of his dark head.

The passenger door opened, and a tall, slender man climbed down. He turned, looked up at Julie on the loading dock and smiled.

Julie stared. She felt as if her knees might suddenly give way on her. Standing there smiling at her was, without question, the handsomest man she had ever seen.

His hair was thick and longish, but obviously styled by an expert hand. His eyes were a startling blue—not a pale blue like Mike's, but a vivid, compelling blue—and the eyelashes that lined them were so thick that they gave his eyes a sexy, almost sulky look. His mouth was wide, the lower lip sensual and generous. His features were almost perfectly even, but his quirky, mischievous smile saved his face from the coldness of perfection. He was older than she had envisioned from what Mike had said about him. She had expected a college boy or at most a man in his early twenties. But this man was more likely in his late twenties or perhaps thirty. His face had the formed handsomeness of maturity, the faint etchings of experience and knowledge that made him much more alluring than a boy.

Julie had never experienced such an immediate and physical response at seeing a man. Her stomach was suddenly jumping with nerves. She found it difficult to breathe, and heat blossomed low in her abdomen. She couldn't look away from him, though she was sure she must look like an idiot staring at him the way she was.

"Good afternoon, ma'am," he said in a voice that had the softness of the South in it and none of the twang of Texas.

"Hello."

Behind her, she heard Mike make an exasperated noise under his breath; then he came forward to stand beside Julie on the dock. "I'll only be a minute, Mr. Marshall. No need for you to get out."

"Oh, but there was a need." The man grinned again. It was impossible not to return that appealing smile. "I wanted to meet this young lady. I'm Taggart Marshall...."

He came up the steps beside the loading dock, his steps a little unsteady, and held out his hand toward Julie. She moved forward to meet him, extending her own hand to shake his. "I'm Julie Farrell."

His hand closed around hers, large and strong-boned, and the heat in her abdomen mushroomed. But at the same instant the smell of Bourbon enveloped her, and she realized that Taggart Marshall was weaving slightly as he stood in front of her, his eyes glazed as they looked down into hers.

Here in the afternoon, in broad daylight no less, this man was thoroughly drunk!

Chapter 2

Julie pulled her hand out of Tag's grasp and said coolly, "It's nice to meet you."

His grin was a little lopsided and very appealing. "I can say—in complete honesty, for once—that the pleasure is all mine."

Julie pushed all thoughts of Marshall's good looks out of her mind and turned back to loading the sacks. The man was falling-down drunk in the middle of the day. Was he an alcoholic? She recalled the things Mike had said about him yesterday. He was a black sheep. He'd been banished to the ranch because of his bad behavior. That was why she had assumed he was younger. What kind of a thirty-year-old man would go wherever his father decided to send him? Would allow his father to administer punishment to him? One who was weak and completely dependent on his father for money. In other words, someone who didn't work but lived on his family's wealth. And if his father was the kind who was content to let a grown son live off him, what must this Taggart Marshall have done that would have made his father so angry? It must have been something pretty reprehensible.

So he was wild, drunk, lazy, weak—and no doubt used to using those blazing good looks and the charm of his smile to get him out of all kinds of scrapes. Why, until she'd realized he was drunk, she'd been about to fall all over him herself. It was a good thing her common sense had returned in time.

Taggart followed her. "Here, let me get that. It's too heavy for you." He reached for the sack, but Granddad quickly picked up the other end and helped her swing it into the truck.

"I'm used to it," Julie said shortly and continued to load. "And I'm better dressed for it." She glanced pointedly at his suit, elegantly cut and doubtless extremely expensive.

He glanced down at his attire and made a wry face. "I didn't come well-prepared, did I? Sorry."

"I'm almost through here, Mr. Marshall," Mike said, taking his arm and steering him back to the steps and down them. "Why don't you wait for me in the truck? You'll be more comfortable there."

Taggart looked at Mike oddly, then turned to face Julie. "Good afternoon, Julie. It was a pleasure to meet you. I hope I'll see you again soon."

"I'm sure we'll run into each other around town," she replied uncomfortably.

He strolled back to the cab and stood leaning against it, casually glancing around him. Mike rejoined Julie and her grandfather, grimacing as he walked toward them. When he reached them, Mike murmured, "He was like that when he got off the plane. Drunk as a skunk. In fact, he was worse then. At least he's had an hour to sober up."

"I can see why his father decided to exile him to the ranch," Julie commented.

"Yeah, I guess he must be a lush," Mike replied.

Julie glanced at Taggart Marshall, and a small sigh escaped her. What a terrible waste.

"How do you know he is a lush?" Vicky Kowalski asked as Julie locked the door of her car and they began to walk toward the bleachers.

"Vicky..." Julie shot the other woman an exasperated glance. Vicky had been her best friend since the first grade, but there were times when she could be distinctly annoying, especially when she was husband-hunting for Julie. She was as eager as Granddad for Julie to meet the right man—though she disagreed that that man was Mike Kubiak—but she was far more wide-ranging and persistent in her matchmaking efforts. "You just don't want to lose another prospective husband for me."

"That's not true!" Vicky turned wide, innocent brown eyes on her. She was a small, attractive girl with the dark coloring of all the Kowalskis, and she had an infectious good-humored, bubbly personality. She was quite different from the quieter, more serious Julie, but their natures had always balanced well. Julie was closer to her than to anyone else, except her sisters and brothers. "But it seems to me that you ought to give the poor man a chance. I mean, you've only met him once. And you did say he was terribly good-looking."

"Well, he was. He is. But he also stank of bourbon. Mike said he'd been drunk as could be when he got off the plane."

"Well, I've known even you, St. Julia of Brinkman, to imbibe a little."

"Not in the middle of the day. If he was drunk when he got off the plane, he must have started drinking in the morning."

"You don't know but what it was a one-time thing. I mean, he might not necessarily drink like a fish all day every day. Maybe he was trying to drown his sorrows about having to live in Brinkman. That'd be enough to drive anybody to drink." Vicky was fond of joking about what a hick town Brinkman was, even though Julie knew that she wouldn't have dreamed of living anywhere else.

"Oh, Vicky! You're just desperate to find me someone to date, that's all. Admit it."

"There is a certain shortage of eligible bachelors in Brinkman," Vicky admitted.

They reached the small wooden shack where the tickets were sold, and Julie stepped up to buy one. "Hi, Alma," she greeted the large black woman inside the booth. Alma was the mother of the team's biggest and most talented lineman, as well as one of the driving forces of the parents' organization. "How's Lonnie tonight?"

"Hi, Julie." Alma flashed Julie a grin as she handed her one of the tickets. "He better be good, that's all I've got to say. After the way he let those little rich boys from the Panhandle push him around last season at the championships...!"

Julie chuckled. It wasn't hard to see where Lonnie Harmon got his competitive spirit. She pushed through the turnstile, with Vicky on her heels, and they walked over to the bleachers.

"Nice crowd tonight," Vicky commented, her eyes scanning the area.

Julie glanced at her, amused. She knew that Vicky was far less interested in the number of townspeople at the football game than she was in the presence of one particular person. "I told him we were going to be here tonight."

Vicky feigned disinterest. "Told who?"

"Told who?" Julie mimicked. "Mike Kubiak, that's who. The man you're looking for."

"I was not looking for Mike Kubiak." Vicky started up the steps.

They were greeted from one side and the other all the way up the steps to an empty bench. Both of the women had lived here all their lives. Vicky taught these people's children at the high school, and Julie sold them the seed for their crops and the feed for their cattle. Between the two of them, there was hardly a person in town they didn't know.

Vicky sat down on the hard wooden bench and asked casually, "Did Mike say he was coming to the game?"

Julie grinned. "I got the impression he might."

Vicky smiled, too. She turned her attention to the field. "Coach says Jackie Ludlow's really improved this year. I hope he's improved his study habits, too, or he won't be playing after six weeks. Thank God he's not in any of my classes. I'd hate to be the one to have to flunk him."

Vicky loved football. In that regard she was like most of the other teachers in the school, as well as most of the townspeople. On Friday evenings half the people in and around Brinkman could be found at the stadium, and when an away game was scheduled, the little town was almost deserted.

Personally, Julie was less interested in football than she was in the game as a social event. While Vicky studied the program and watched the players warming up, all the time making comments as to this student's skill or that one's progress, Julie watched the parade of people pass the bleachers and listened to snatches of conversation floating through the air.

"Hey, Sonny, how's it going?"

"Can't complain."

"... never been the same since he came back from the hospital in Houston."

"You remember Willie, he was John Warshinski's son by his second wife, the one from over around Westphalia."

She saw Cathy walk by, giggling with a group of her girlfriends, and some time later she saw Riley strolling along, his hand intertwined with Susie Whalen's.

A few minutes later she spotted Mike Kubiak. She also saw that right behind him was the tall dark man who had been with him at the store the other day. She was astonished to see that Taggart looked even more handsome than he had the first time she saw him. He also looked, in his flawless, expensive slacks and pullover shirt, as out of place as a movie star among the rougher jeaned and booted farmers.

Julie poked Vicky in the ribs with her elbow. "There's Mike. And he brought that Marshall guy with him."

Vicky turned to look and her eyes widened. For once her attention was not wholly concentrated on Mike Kubiak. "Oh, my..." She rolled her eyes toward Julie. "You didn't do him justice. That man is gorgeous. I think if I were you I'd give him a second chance."

"I'm sure people usually do," Julie commented dryly.

"Don't be such a Puritan."

"I'm not. He's a rich, spoiled playboy, and I have no intention of getting mixed up with him."

"You could tell all this after talking to him for two minutes?" Vicky asked skeptically, still studying Taggart Marshall as he and Mike scanned the stands. "Gee, Jule, you usually aren't judgmental. Why are you being so hard on this guy?"

"I'm not," Julie protested. Yet she suspected that if it had been any other man she probably wouldn't have been as quick to label him. There seemed to be an instinctive sort of self-defense at work inside her. Almost as if she had sensed that this man could hurt her, and that only by setting him aside in a category of forbidden men would she keep her heart safe from him.

It was Taggart who spotted them first. Julie saw the smile of recognition light up his face. Beside her, Vicky drew in her breath sharply. "And a heartbreaker smile, too! Oh, Julie! This man is dangerous. Who cares about his vices?"

Taggart nudged Mike and said something to him, and Mike looked up. He raised a hand in a wave, and Julie offered a weak smile. Vicky made a beckoning motion, pointing to the empty seats beside them, and the two men began to climb the bleacher steps. Julie watched them, her attention focusing on the smooth, easy movement of Taggart's long legs. Her mouth felt dry, and her heart was pounding in double time. Mentally she cursed herself for acting this way. She never went gaga over any man. Why on earth would she feel vulnerable and shaky now, with someone who was so obviously wrong for her?

She was glad she had arranged it so that Vicky sat beside the empty seats, not her. But when Taggart Marshall sat next to Vicky, shaking her hand and smiling down into her dazzled face as Mike introduced them, Julie was aware of a sharp stab of jealousy. No, it wasn't jealousy. It couldn't be, she told herself. She was just irritated because Taggart was ruining her plan. She had meant for Mike to sit next to Vicky.

"Well, you're certainly getting a taste of small town Texas," Vicky told Taggart.

His blue eyes glinted devilishly, and a dimple flashed in his cheek. "It *is* interesting," he said, glancing around the small stadium.

"It's *the* social gathering of the week in Brinkman," Vicky told him.

Julie felt like jabbing her friend with her elbow, and she probably would have—if it wouldn't have been so obvious. She'd intended for Vicky to have a chance to talk and flirt with Mike, not Taggart Marshall. And there wasn't any reason for her to sound so snide about Brinkman's provincialism. Vicky got as excited as any of them about the football games.

"Brinkman's gone to the state championships in Class A for the past two years, and four years ago they were the state champs," Mike said, explaining the popularity of the games. Julie thought that Mike didn't look pleased, either, which made her feel a little better about the situation. Maybe Mike would begin to get interested in Vicky if he thought she was interested in another man.

"It's part of the tradition of this town," Julie added. "Brinkman's always been good in football. I think it's one of the things that's kept it alive when so many other small towns are dying."

Vicky looked somewhat taken aback by the others' vigorous defense of football, and a momentary silence fell upon the group.

Julie jumped to her feet. "I'm going to get a drink. Anyone want anything? Soda? Popcorn?"

Vicky blinked. "Now?" She looked toward the end of the field, where the cheerleaders and band were lining up on either side of the goalposts, forming a spirit corridor for the players to run through when they came on the field. "But the game's just about to start."

"That's okay." This was the best time for her to leave Vicky and Mike alone, not counting their city-bred guest. Mike was crazy about football, and he wouldn't volunteer to join her at the snack bar right before the kickoff. "I don't mind missing the beginning."

Vicky shrugged. "Okay. Why don't you bring me a cola?"

Tag rose lithely from the bench. "I'll go with you," he offered. "To help you carry the stuff back."

"Okay." His accompanying her would facilitate her scheme to throw Mike and Vicky together, but Julie wasn't sure she wanted him to go with her, even so. She found his presence altogether too unsettling.

Julie slipped past the others to the steps. Her body brushed lightly against Tag's as she went by, and she felt the small contact in every nerve of her body. This was crazy, she thought. The way she was acting, you would think she was some high school girl who'd never been around a man.

Taggart exited after her and followed her down the metal steps to the bottom of the bleachers. Julie moved quickly, not glancing back to see if he was with her. He caught up with her as they left the bleachers, his long legs easily matching her stride.

"You must be in a real hurry to get back," he commented as Julie strode toward the refreshment stand.

"What? Oh. No, not really." She forced herself to slow down. "Sorry. I had my mind on something else."

They met several people on their way to the refreshment stand, and nearly all of them greeted Julie happily. Carla Forman, whose son was in FFA with Cathy, stopped to chat about the upcoming animal show. Tag waited patiently, his arms crossed, a faint smile on his lips.

"Do you know everybody?" he teased, when Julie finished the conversation with Mrs. Forman and turned away.

Julie smiled a little. "Not quite. There are a few people I don't know. People who don't have kids in high school, go to our church, or buy feed or seed."

"I take it that eliminates most of the people in town."

Julie nodded. "Yeah. I've lived here all my life, and before that so did my parents. And before that, so did my grandfather. In fact, his grandparents moved to this county in the late 1800s."

"You like it here, don't you?"

She glanced at him, her chin coming up a little. "Of course I do. You sound surprised. I take it you don't like Brinkman?"

He shrugged. "I don't know. I haven't been here long enough to decide. That wasn't why I was surprised. I always assumed young people were eager to *leave* small towns."

"They are. When I went off to college, I wanted to get away from all the people knowing your business and the gossip and the lack of entertainment. But it didn't take me long to realize that those things aren't half as bad as being alone and homesick. I guess I'm just a small town girl at heart." Julie imagined that Tag thought she was provincial and dull. But that was just as well. He had seemed interested in her the other day, and she didn't want him to be.

They reached the refreshment stand, and Julie purchased soft drinks and popcorn, chatting with the women behind the counter, who were also good customers at her store. She could feel Taggart Marshall's eyes on her, and it made her nervous. What was he thinking?

She was very conscious of her usual casual outfit of jeans and a shirt, and she wished that she had at least put on a more attractive top instead of the plain red cotton shirt. He probably thought she was a real hick, and much as she told herself that she didn't care—was glad, even—the truth of the matter was that it bothered her.

Tag Marshall stood to one side of the line in front of the refreshment stand, studying the rear view of Julie's figure. It was a nice view, he thought. She was one of those rare women who could wear jeans well, neither fat nor skinny, with nicely rounded hips that made a man think about smoothing his hands over them. He had never been around a woman quite like her before—no more than he'd lived anyplace quite like Brinkman, Texas. But Tag Marshall was a man who was always open to new experiences.

When he'd decided to come to the family ranch, he hadn't expected to meet someone like Julie Farrell. Even less would he have expected to be attracted to her. But the moment he'd seen her slim, jean-clad figure the other day, his heart had begun to pick up its beat and his blood to course a little hotter in his veins. He'd known he wouldn't rest until he knew her better.

Her face had been almost devoid of makeup, and her curling chestnut brown hair had been pulled back and caught in a plain, practical way. But there was something about her strong-boned face that was arresting, almost exotic, and her skin was so fresh and creamy smooth that it had been all he could do not to reach out and touch her cheek. He had been aware of a strong urge to unclasp the barrette that held back her hair, uncoil her single braid and plunge his fingers into the thick, soft mass. Julie had a warm, natural kind of beauty that needed no artifice, and though Tag had never dated a woman who didn't look as if she'd just stepped out of an Elizabeth Arden salon—with a side trip into a designer boutique—he found this woman's very difference exciting.

However, she seemed to have no interest in him, a situation Tag had never encountered before. It wasn't that he was vain about his looks and charm, but he wasn't stupid, either. He was fully aware of the way women usually responded to him, and Julie Farrell's indifference both surprised and intrigued him.

Behind the refreshment counter, a woman with black hair and the squarish, strong-jawed face he'd seen on so many people in this town, handed Julie a cardboard tray of drinks and popcorn, then grinned at the man who stepped up to the counter after Julie and cried something that sounded like, "Stash! *Yok che mosh!* When're you coming back home to stay?"

Tag took the tray from Julie. "Was that woman speaking a foreign language?"

Julie looked puzzled and glanced back toward the refreshment stand. Then she smiled, her face clearing. "Oh. Yeah. I didn't even pay any attention. It's Polish—some kind of greeting. Mike or Vicky would know. That's Stash Kowalski she was talking to. He's one of Vicky's cousins. Half the town is Vicky's cousins."

"Are there a lot of Polish-Americans here? Somehow that doesn't sound like Texas."

Julie chuckled. "Oh, sure. And Czechs. Some Germans. This whole area is full of little Central European communities. I don't know why they originally settled here, exactly. But I guess Brinkman is about half Polish and Czech descendants. The rest of us are blacks or Wasps."

"Interesting place."

Julie glanced at him, uncertain whether he was being serious or sarcastic, and her eyes met his bright blue gaze. She felt a funny melting sensation in the area of her stomach that was becoming all too familiar. It annoyed her that she should feel this way about a man who was obviously more charm than substance. She had always thought of herself as a solid, down-to-earth person, someone who wasn't swayed by good looks or money or a grin that could light up a room. It annoyed her to discover that she was as vulnerable as the next woman.

"Julie..." Tag stopped, and she paused, too.

"Yes?" She struggled to keep both her gaze and her voice cool. She might feel the effect of his smile, but she wasn't about to let it show.

"I wanted to ask you..." He paused, and she thought she saw a flash of uncertainty in his eyes. Then he went on. "Are you free tomorrow night? I'd like to take you out. Maybe we could go to Austin for a movie or dinner."

"I can't," Julie said flatly. She realized that her response sounded rude, and she fumbled around for some way to soften it. "That is, well, I have plans."

"Perhaps another time?"

She shifted uncomfortably. "I don't think so. I really don't date very much."

"You don't date? You mean, you're seeing someone?"

"No. But I don't have the time. Dating's for kids."

His eyebrows lifted. "Oh, I see. And you, of course, are too old."

Julie blushed, feeling foolish. "Of course not. But I'm too busy. I don't have the time or the interest. I'm sorry. That's just the way I am."

"Or as least the way you are about me."

"I don't know what you mean."

"I get the distinct impression that you don't like me."

"I don't know you."

"And obviously don't want to."

Julie cocked an eyebrow in exasperation. "Are you always this persistent?"

"No. Generally I take rejection quite graciously. But you seem, well, almost hostile. Have I offended you somehow?"

"Mr. Marshall..."

"Tag."

"Tag, I'm sure you're accustomed to women falling all over you, and it must seem strange that I haven't. But I'm simply not all that interested in either dating or you. Frankly, I can't see why you want to go out with me. We have nothing in common. You'll be going back home soon. We—"

"How do you know all these things? You've hardly spoken to me. How would you know when I'm returning to North Carolina or whether or not we have anything in common?"

"I think it's pretty obvious. You don't belong here."

His eyes narrowed. "Does everyone around here have as big a chip on their shoulder as you do? Are you automatically ostracized if your parents and your grandparents didn't grow up in Brinkman?"

"Of course not." Julie set her mouth. "It has nothing to do with where you're from. Look at the facts. This is a plain, hardworking rural community. You're a wealthy, idle city boy. The two just don't mix."

"I see. So I've already been tried and hanged. Is that it?"

Julie looked startled. "No. I meant—"

"How about if I bought a cowboy hat and boots?"

"Oh, for—" Julie glanced at him and saw that his eyes were twinkling, and she couldn't help but laugh. "Would you cut it out?"

"What?" He looked injured and innocent. "I was simply asking a legitimate question."

"Sure."

"Well, I was."

"You were making fun of me."

"Never," he assured her, a comic hand over his heart. "Make fun of a woman who won't date a man because he's from the city? How could I?"

"That is not what I said."

"Oh, that's right. *And* because I have money." He grinned. "Now, there's a heinous crime. I've been turned down before because of it. A lot of women go for abject poverty."

A gurgle of laughter escaped her. "Stop it." This man was altogether too appealing. Here she'd just turned him down, and now he was making her laugh.

They climbed the steps to their row. Both Vicky and Mike were absorbed in the game, barely glancing up when Julie and Tag sidled over. The other two took their drinks and a bag of popcorn and returned to the game, talking earnestly about the merits of the other team's defense.

Julie smiled to herself. Her matchmaking scheme seemed to be working. This time she had maneuvered it so that Tag had gone down the bench first, putting him next to Mike and her on the end. She settled down to watch the game, one eye on Vicky and Mike.

When the game ended and they left the bleachers, Mike and Vicky walked along together, absorbed in a discussion of the various key plays of the game and the efforts of the players. "Why don't we go to the Kustard Korner and get an ice cream?" Mike asked cheerfully.

Julie shot a glance at Tag. She wondered what he must think about the nightlife Brinkman had to offer. "No," she said. "I can't. I have to get up early tomorrow to open the store. But why don't you all go ahead?"

Mike hesitated. "Oh. Okay." He turned toward Vicky. "How about it, Vicky? Tag and I can drop you off afterward."

"Sure." They split up, heading toward their respective cars, waving a goodbye to each other. As the walked off, Vicky turned to look back at Julie and grinned at her broadly.

Julie smiled, too, satisfied that her plan had succeeded. She walked on to her car, wondering why, since things had worked out just as she had wanted them to, she was feeling so deflated. She got into her car, turned on the ignition and lights, and pulled out into the line of cars leaving the stadium. And why, she thought as she waited in line, with all the friends and family she had, did she suddenly feel alone and blue?

Julie saw Tag Marshall again the following week. She was outside helping her grandfather unload sacks of feed from the truck, and he was driving down the main street past her store in the Mercedes that was always kept on the ranch for the owners' use. She also noticed that there was a redheaded woman in the front seat beside him. She grimaced. It hadn't taken him long to find someone more willing than she was. Julie didn't recognize her, and she wondered if she were someone Tag had met in Austin. No doubt he drove up there frequently, bored with life in Brinkman.

The next time Mike came into the store she pumped him gently for information. He was only too glad to have something to talk about with her.

"Oh, yeah," he said, nodding. "Taggart's got company staying at the ranch this week. His guests flew in from North Carolina on Sunday. I don't know how long they're planning on staying. But Helen's mad as all get out 'cause that redhead's real finicky about what she eats. She turned up her nose at the sausage from Kowalski's store, said it was like asking for clogged arteries. Well, you know Helen. She's Joe Kowalski's cousin, and she didn't take that too well. She says the woman's got to have one egg, poached, every morning, and a slice of toast. Whole wheat, just a certain shade of brown.''

Mike laughed. ''So Helen comes to me, and she says she doesn't mind cooking for 'that Marshall guy,' as well as keeping house, seeing as how he's just one person—frankly, I think he charmed the socks off her—but there's no way she's going to continue to cook for that 'devil woman' and her two friends.''

Julie laughed. ''What did you do?''

''I told her to tell Taggart. I figured it was his problem, anyway. I guess he calmed Helen down, 'cause she's still cooking, and the redhead's still there.''

''Is she his girlfriend?''

''I suppose. I don't know. She came with two men.''

She must have a serious relationship with Tag to fly all the way from North Carolina just to visit him when he's been gone only a week, thought Julie. Imagine Taggart asking her out when he had a serious girlfriend back home—and when that girlfriend was coming to visit him a few days later, too! It was insulting to both of them.

She had been right in labeling him a playboy, she thought, and she was glad that she hadn't let him charm her into going out with him. Tag Marshall would be nothing but heartbreak.

Chapter 3

Julie slid in the last plate, poured in the detergent and closed the dishwasher. She turned the dial to On, then turned and surveyed the kitchen. Riley had cleaned the table and swept the floor—his chores this week—and he hadn't done too sloppy a job, even though he had rushed through it so he could get ready for his date. She walked over to the table and pushed one of the chairs all the way in just as heavy footsteps sounded on the steps outside and Cathy flung open the back door in her usual impetuous manner. She had been down to the pen to feed her show steer.

"Clown's looking great," she said, flopping down at the kitchen table and propping her feet up on another chair. "I bet he'll take Grand Champion at the County Fair this year."

Julie smiled. "Pretty sure of yourself, aren't you?"

Cathy shrugged. "That's what it takes."

Julie opened a drawer and pulled out a pile of envelopes and a calculator, then set them down on the kitchen table. Cathy looked at the envelopes and made an expression of disgust.

"Bills? That's how you're going to spend your Friday night? Paying bills?"

"That's right." Julie added a checkbook to the pile on the table and sat down. "Good a time as any." Between running the business and the house, time was always at a premium with her. Even though Riley and Cathy were pretty good at helping out with the chores, it seemed that there was always something to be cleaned or mended or cooked. Then there were all the school activities she had to attend, since Mom and Dad weren't there to do it, as well as the various community events she needed to go to because of the business.

Horace came into the kitchen while she was writing out checks. He had on his best Western shirt, gray with maroon piping and gray slacks. His cowboy boots were polished to a shine. In his hand he carried his gray felt Stetson, which he only wore when he was dressed up.

"Mmm, you smell good," Julie said, sniffing the air appreciatively. "You must have a hot date tonight."

Horace grinned. "Riette and I are going dancing at the SPJST Hall in Horton," he said, referring to one of the large family-oriented dance halls in the area operated by a Czech/American organization.

He nodded and executed a dance step. "That woman sure loves to dance."

"Granddad, you kill me." Cathy grinned. "Don't you know you're supposed to stay at home and rock and smoke a pipe and talk about your rheumatiz?"

Horace cackled. "Me? You're crazy, girl. I've never had rheumatism in my life. If I did, I sure wouldn't talk about it."

"Are you going to stay out all night again?" Cathy asked drolly, her eyes twinkling.

"Cathy!"

"Oh, Jule, get real." Cathy rolled her eyes. "As if we didn't all know what Granddad and Riette do after they go out honky-tonking."

"Now you keep a civil tongue in your head, young lady," Horace told her sternly. "Especially when you're talking about Miss Riette."

"'Miss Riette'?" Cathy giggled. "Oh, Granddad, I love it when you get all Southern gentleman on me." She jumped up to kiss her grandfather on the cheek.

Horace looked gratified, though he did his best to hide it with a frown. "Don't think you can—"

His words were interrupted by the squeal of tires on the road in front of their house. He stopped in midsentence, and the three of them looked at each other. Horace turned and started toward the front of the house out of idle curiosity, and Julie and Cathy trailed after him. Just as he reached the front door to look out, there was a thunderous pounding on it. He jerked the door open.

Julie's mouth dropped open. Standing outside was Tag Marshall. He was dressed in a tuxedo and looked unbelievably handsome, but there was a palpable sense of distress and haste about him that was at odds with his neat, sophisticated look.

"I'm sorry. Do you have a dog?" he said as soon as Granddad opened the door. Then his eyes went past the older man and fell on Julie. His eyes widened. "Oh. You. I—do you have a black-and-white dog?"

"Jackson?" Julie joined her grandfather in the doorway and looked past Tag toward the highway. A beige Mercedes sat in the road, its blinkers flashing, and Julie could discern the outline of a woman sitting in the front passenger seat. On the shoulder of the road lay a black-and-white bundle. "Jackson!"

Fear clutched her heart, and she shoved past her grandfather and Tag. She ran to the highway, only dimly aware of Tag running after her, and dropped down onto her knees beside the dog lying on the shoulder of the road. "Jackson!"

There was blood all over Jackson's head and shoulders, matting his fur. But his eyes were open, and when she bent over him, he lifted his head slightly and his tail twitched.

"I'm sorry, Julie. God, I'm so sorry." Tag dropped down beside her on his knees. He was peeling off his tuxedo jacket as he talked. "I didn't see him. I tried to stop. But all of a sudden, there he was in the road."

Tears blinded her eyes. "I know. He's bad about running out. He thinks he owns the road."

Gently Taggart spread his jacket over the dog. He pulled out a handkerchief and pressed it to Jackson's head. "Most of the blood's coming from this gash on his head. Where's the vet? Maybe if we get him there in time..."

"Of course." Julie blinked the tears away. There was no time to waste crying. It wouldn't do Jackson any good. She reached out to slide her hands under the dog to pick him up, but Tag was already doing that.

"I'll get him. He's heavy. Run and open the back door."

Julie jumped up and hurried to do as he said. Behind her, Tag slowly picked the dog up and rose, being careful not to jar him. Julie was afraid that in his pain Jackson might bite a stranger, but he didn't. As Tag carried him carefully to the car the front door opened and a red-haired woman stepped out.

She was pretty, dressed in a beautiful long gown, a diamond pendant winking at her throat. But her loveliness was marred by the frown that wrinkled her forehead and the narrow line of her compressed lips. "Tag! What in the world are you doing? If we don't leave now, we'll be late!"

Tag didn't even glance at her. "I'm taking this dog to the vet, Marilyn."

"The vet!" Her voice quivered with outrage. "Tag! This ball is one of *the* events of the year in Austin. We can't miss it just for a dog!"

Tag motioned to Julie to get into the car, and she slid into the back seat and across to the middle. Tag leaned in, laying Jackson on the back seat, his head in Julie's lap.

"That's your jacket!" The other woman gasped in horrified tones as she saw what Jackson was wrapped in. "And there's blood on your shirt."

Cathy and Horace had followed them out to the car and were standing, watching helplessly. "Honey, you want me to follow you?" Horace asked.

"No, you go on and see Riette. It's okay. Just call Dr. Samuelson and tell him we're coming. He's probably already closed for the day."

"I'll bring her back," Tag promised as he closed the door and went around to the driver's side. "Marilyn, either get in the car or close the door. We have to go." He jumped in and started the engine.

"Tag! I am not going to the vet's in my brand new—"

None too gently, Cathy reached out and took the woman's arm, pulled her aside and slammed the door. Tag made a U-turn and took off, leaving the redhead standing beside Cathy, staring open-mouthed after them.

Tag jammed down on the accelerator, and the powerful car responded smoothly. Julie pressed the handkerchief to Jackson's head, and the big dog whimpered. She spoke soothingly to him, her free hand gently stroking his hindquarters.

"You'll have to give me directions," Tag said from the front seat.

"Just stay on this road. He's right at the edge of town on the right-hand side. It's a gray cement block building, one-story, with a big parking lot. There's always a blue horse trailer parked beside it."

"What about the vet? Will it take him long to get there?"

"No. He lives next door to his clinic so he can check on the animals. He'll go over and set up as soon as Granddad calls him."

They flew down the road, taking the curves with ease. Tag drove skillfully, as well as quickly.

"I'm sorry," he said again. "I didn't see him in time."

"I know. We heard you try to stop. It's not your fault."

"I feel terrible about it."

"Don't. It's something that happens when you live near a road. One of our other dogs died like that. It's just that Jackson is so special." Her voice quavered and broke on the words. "I got him for my birthday when I was thirteen." She bent her head over the dog's, tears splashing down onto his muzzle. His tail stirred faintly.

"He has a chance," Tag said firmly. "I really think he has a chance. I was able to slow down and turn enough so just the corner of the bumper caught him."

"Sure. He has a chance." Julie wiped the tears from her eyes and turned her attention to the road. They were nearing Brinkman. "It's not much farther now. There. See it up ahead? That long, low building?"

"Yeah." He slowed down and made a careful turn into the potholed parking lot. He stopped the car, then hurried around to lift Jackson out.

Julie jumped out and ran to open the clinic door for him. Dr. Samuelson stood waiting for them in the doorway to one of the examination rooms. "In here," he said tersely as Tag carried Jackson inside.

Tag laid the dog down on the metal table, and the veterinarian peeled away the jacket and handkerchief to look at the wounds. Dr. Samuelson's wife, Marie, bustled into the room, a white lab coat buttoned over her dress, high heels on her feet. Obviously they had been on their way out when Horace's call had interrupted them.

"Here now, Julie," she said in a motherly tone, curling an arm around Julie and giving her a reassuring squeeze. "I'll help Donald. You just go on outside and sit down."

Julie nodded. She wasn't the best person to help right now. She was usually able to doctor the farm's animals without squeamishness, but Jackson was different. The pain and patience in his golden eyes tore at her heart.

Tag put his arm around Julie and led her from the room, closing the door behind him. She leaned into him, beginning to tremble with the aftermath of shock and adrenaline. He wrapped his other arm around her and held her close. His arms were strong, his chest comfortingly hard and warm. Julie clung to him for a moment, fighting the sobs that threatened to overwhelm her.

"It's okay." He gently rubbed her back. "You can cry."

"I don't cry," she choked out, then belied her words by bursting into tears.

He held her while she cried. And, somehow, holding on to him like that, her face buried in his chest, it didn't hurt as much to cry. Gradually her sobs quieted and her arms relaxed around him. For a long moment after she had stopped crying she simply stood, resting against Tag. But then, with a sigh, she let her arms fall away and stepped back.

"I'm sorry." She wiped the tears from her cheeks.

"I'd offer you my handkerchief, but I'm afraid we used it on your dog."

"It's okay. I have some tissues in my purse." She stopped. "Oh, darn. I don't even have my purse."

She went over to the receptionist's counter and found a box of tissues. She wiped her eyes and blew her nose, then went down the hall to the bathroom and splashed a little water on her face. By the time she returned she felt almost normal again, except for worrying about Jackson. The situation didn't seem as bleak or as frightening as it had a few minutes earlier. Tag was right. Since Jackson hadn't been hit full speed and head on, there was a chance he would make it.

Tag was standing looking out the front window, but he turned at the sound of her footsteps on the linoleum floor and smiled. "You look like you feel a little better."

"Thanks. I do." She tried an answering smile. "I'm sorry for crying all over you like that."

"No need to apologize. I didn't mind."

"I'm not usually so weepy. But Jackson—well, I've had him a long time, and my parents gave him to me."

He walked over to her. "Of course he's special to you. There's nothing wrong with crying over a dog."

They sat down to wait. The minutes seemed to stretch on endlessly. After a while Julie got up and began to pace the length of the room. It didn't help her nerves. She kept thinking about Jackson. Worrying.

She stopped at the end of the waiting room and looked back at Tag. He sat far down in the chair, his legs stretched out in front of him and his head resting against the wall. He had untied his bow tie and unbuttoned the top button of his shirt. His eyes were closed. Under her regard he opened his eyes and turned his head.

"What? Is something the matter?"

"No." She shook her head. "I was just thinking that it's a shame you're stuck here. I should have brought my car. I wasn't thinking. But Granddad's already gone, and Cathy doesn't have a license. She can't come get me."

"It's okay. I don't mind waiting. Besides, I want to know how he does."

"Thank you. I guess your date's ruined. I'm sorry."

He shrugged. "Don't worry. I'll live. It wasn't that big a deal, anyway. I've been to hundreds of charity galas before, and I don't even know the people at this one. It was Marilyn's idea. Some sorority sister of hers is from Austin."

"Perhaps you ought to go get her. She won't like waiting this long at our house."

He grinned, mischief sparking in his eyes. "You're right about that. But I called one of the guys who came with Marilyn while you were in the bathroom and told him what happened. He and Lane are going to run over there and pick her up. I got your number from the book and called Marilyn and told her." He chuckled. "She gave me an earful."

"I'm sorry."

He shook his head. "Don't worry about it. I've heard worse."

"Still, it's ruined your evening, and it wasn't your fault."

"Like I said, it's not that big a deal."

Julie glanced at the clock on the wall. "How long have we been here?"

"Less than an hour, I'd say."

"It seems like forever." She resumed her pacing.

A few minutes later the door to the examination room opened and the veterinarian emerged. Julie looked at him, and hope began to flutter in her chest. He didn't look unhappy. In fact, he was smiling a little.

"Well, Julie," he said, "I think you have one lucky dog."

"He's going to be okay?"

"I think so."

"Oh, Dr. Samuelson! That's wonderful!" A grin burst across her face. She looked at Tag, and he grinned back at her. She crossed the room to Dr. Samuelson, and Tag rose and joined her.

"I couldn't detect any internal injuries. I think it must have been only a glancing blow."

"Thank God." Tag let out a sigh of relief.

"He has a nasty cut on his head, but it looks worse than it is, and Jackson was never a beauty to begin with. His leg is broken and he has some cracked ribs, too. I taped him up, and I think he should be all right. Just in case, though, I'd like him to stay the night so I can keep an eye on him."

"Of course." Julie felt like hugging the staid vet, but she knew he would probably be dismayed by such a display of emotion. Tag put his arm around her shoulders and squeezed, and Julie turned gratefully and hugged him. His body was hard and warm beneath her arms; she could hear the thud of his heart beneath her ear. It felt good to be held by him. She thought of snuggling into him and staying that way. When she realized what she was thinking, Julie pulled away abruptly and stepped back, her face flaming with embarrassment.

Tag paid the vet over Julie's protestations that it was her responsibility, and they left the animal clinic and drove back to her house in silence. She felt suddenly drained and tired.

Tag stopped the car in front of the house and walked her to the door. Tired as she was, she found that she was reluctant to let him leave. "Would you like to come in? I could fix us some coffee or something."

"Okay." Tag followed her inside.

Julie wondered what he thought of their plain old farmhouse. The porch sagged a little, and the whole place needed to be repainted. It had been built by her great grandfather and added onto by each succeeding generation, so that, although fairly large, it was a sprawling hodge-podge of styles. There never seemed to be enough time or money to really fix it up. It was warmly familiar and beloved to Julie, but she suspected that Tag was used to something far more magnificent. She was intensely aware of the scuffed hardwood floors in the hallway and the cracked, nondescript linoleum in the kitchen. She sneaked a glance at Tag. He was looking around with interest. When his eyes met hers, he grinned.

"This is a real farmhouse, isn't it?"

"Well, yes." She gave him an odd look.

"You probably think I'm crazy. It's just . . . well, it looks so homey and—and natural. It's like something out of a movie."

Julie laughed. "Hardly."

"How old is it?"

"Almost a hundred years. This kitchen is much newer, though. My grandfather built it. And the den on the back used to be a screened-in porch, what they called a sleeping porch. The kids used to sleep there when the weather was warm 'cause it was so much cooler."

Cathy came bouncing into the kitchen to inquire after Jackson, then left them alone, shooting a significant look at Julie. Julie put the coffee on to brew while Tag roamed around the kitchen, poking into all the odd corners and angles.

"My mother has a lot of antique furniture and stuff, but none of it's like this. It's all terribly formal, and you can't touch it. Everything here has been used and loved. None of our houses ever looks like it's been lived in."

"Well, this one's been lived in plenty, I can assure you."

They sat down at the kitchen table and waited for the coffee to be ready.

"I want to thank you for all you did," Julie told him. "It wasn't necessary, and it was very kind of you to do it." She was frankly amazed at how nice he had been. The things he had done tonight didn't seem at all like the actions of some rich, lazy snob from the East.

"You don't need to thank me. I'm just sorry it happened." His blue eyes were warm and friendly, candid.

"A lot of people would figure they'd done enough by stopping and telling us what happened. In fact, I suspect that most people would have just driven on."

"And left your dog suffering?" Tag looked grim. "Is that what you would expect of me?"

"Well, no—I don't know. I hadn't thought about it. But I guess I wouldn't have expected you to be so thoughtful or kind or easy-going about it. I mean, you ruined your jacket, your shirt . . . your date."

He grimaced. "That was no loss."

"Tag!" But she had to grin. She couldn't imagine missing a date with Marilyn to be much of a loss, either.

"Look, I have to apologize for the way Marilyn acted. She was rude and self-centered."

"That's all right. You don't have to apologize for her."

"Yes, I do. She's my responsibility since she's my houseguest."

"I'm sure she must have other qualities—I mean, likable things."

He shrugged. "Oh, she can be fun, I guess, as long as you're doing something she's interested in, which usually means something that revolves around her.

Tonight was a pretty good example of her true nature, I'm afraid." A smile lightened his face. "But maybe she'll get so mad that she'll decide to go home."

Julie stared, a little shocked. "Tag!"

He shrugged. "Well, I didn't ask her to come. She and Kevin and Lane decided to fly over and see me on their own. It was kind of a lark, a spur of the moment thing. Kevin just got his pilot's license, and I guess he was itching to fly somewhere. I wasn't exactly overjoyed to see them."

"Oh." Julie knew she shouldn't be so happy that he wasn't attached to Marilyn, but she was. "I figured maybe she was your girlfriend."

Tag made a face. "Give me some credit."

Julie smiled and got up to pour their coffee. She set the cups down on the table and pulled a milk carton out of the refrigerator. "Want anything in it?"

He glanced at the inelegant container and a tiny grin tugged at his lips. "Sure. Milk and sugar."

She poured a dollop of milk into each cup and set the sugar canister on the table in front of him. She had a creamer and sugar bowl in the cabinet, but something inside her was defiantly determined not to dress anything up just for Taggart Marshall.

They stirred their coffee and sipped it, quiet for a moment.

"Would you answer a question?" he asked finally.

"Sure."

"Why are you so set against me?"

"I'm not!" Julie protested.

He cocked an eyebrow. "You turned me down pretty flat last Friday. And you seemed embarrassingly surprised that I displayed even the most ordinary human decency tonight. I can't help but think you dislike me. Why? Have I done something to offend you?"

Julie felt a blush rising to her cheeks. "No. I'm sorry. It was wrong of me. I misjudged you. Obviously I—well, I assumed things I had no right to assume. I didn't give you a fair shake. I knew that you were wealthy and that you were kind of wild, an embarrassment to your family, and—" She stopped, realizing that she had given away the source of her information. No one else would have known those things except Mike, who had heard them from Tag's father.

"I should have known. No doubt my father fed Mike an earful of interesting information about me and he was only too happy to repeat it."

"Oh, dear." Julie leaned across the table earnestly, stretching out a hand to touch his. "Please, don't be mad at Mike. I'm sure he never would have said anything about it if he thought he had been told in confidence."

"Oh, I don't blame him. Who wouldn't repeat a juicy bit of gossip like that? I'm sure my father didn't say it in confidence. He doesn't give a damn who knows what he thinks about his 'wastrel' son." His voice rang with bitterness. He gave Julie a wry smile, but there was a darkness in his blue eyes that belied any amusement.

"Leith Marshall doesn't believe that the two words 'idle and rich' should ever go together. Not only should a Marshall be a productive member of society, he should also, if at all possible, be an attorney. And I dropped out the first year of law school."

"Oh. But surely he doesn't really think that's the only occupation you could have."

"By this time I think my father would be happy if I decided to be a ditchdigger, so long as I had a job. You see, I also tried working in my uncle's bank, and that lasted less than a year. The Taggarts offered me a position in the mill business, but I didn't accept. I knew I'd never last a day in the textile business. Of course, between the family and its connections, there are probably fifty businesses in North Carolina that I could get a job with, but I've never applied. The truth is, my father's right—I'm lazy and aimless. I don't like books. I don't like business. I don't like to sit at a desk all day."

"There must be something you like to do."

"Sure. Sailing. Riding. Tennis. Parties. But I can't make a career out of any of those. I'm not up to that standard. I take it you agree with my father. You don't approve of a man who lives off his trust funds."

"I don't know. It does seem as though a person ought to do more in life. Of course, most of us don't have any choice. I guess a lot of people wouldn't work if they didn't have to." She hesitated, then said slowly, "But even if you have enough money not to have to work, I would think you could do something more worthwhile than drink and party."

He stared. "That's not *all* I do. Is that what my father said?"

"Well, no, I don't think so. I mean, I'm not sure exactly what he said to Mike. But I got the impression that you were something of a black sheep. Kind of wild. And then when you showed up...I liked you. Obviously you have a kind, warm heart. But it's not good for you to drink like that."

"Drink like what?" He looked puzzled.

Julie drew up her courage. "Like the way you were when you came to town. You have to be awfully close to being an alcoholic to get that drunk in the middle of the day."

To her surprise, Tag's face cleared and he laughed. "Is *that* why you think I'm a lowlife?" He put his head in his hands. His shoulders shook with laughter. "Oh, Lord. There's no way out of this one without embarrassing myself."

He stopped laughing and sighed, straightening up to face her. "Okay. I promise you, I am not a drunk. I don't spend all my time partying and drinking. Nor am I commonly 'inebriated' in the middle of the afternoon." He rubbed his hands across his face. "I had had several drinks on the plane that day. The reason is . . . oh, hell! I'm scared of flying."

Julie's eyes widened. "What!"

"I don't like to fly. It makes me nervous. I often have a drink to settle my nerves. This was a long flight, so I had several."

Julie began to laugh.

Tag rolled his eyes. "I knew it. Now you think I'm an idiot."

"No, I don't. Really." Julie reined in her laughter. "Lots of people are scared to fly. It's just—oh, I don't know. You're such a sophisticated person. I pictured you as jetting casually over to Monte Carlo or maybe up to New York for the weekend to catch a show, or off to some exotic, expensive resort. And here you are, scared of flying. It just seems sort of—"

"Silly," he supplied in a resigned tone. "I know." But there was an amused twinkle in his eye that belied his martyred tone.

He didn't take himself too seriously, and Julie liked that. She liked *him*.

Looking at him sitting there in the crisply pleated tuxedo shirt, open at the throat, she found herself thinking about what it would feel like to kiss the shallow hollow of his throat and have his arms around her, the wide spread of his hand across her back. He was the handsomest man she'd ever met and the *only* one whom just looking at could set her heart to pounding. It was crazy. Pointless. She could think of probably a hundred other negative things to say about even thinking about a guy like Tag Marshall. Still...she couldn't keep from sitting here and wondering.

"So, tell me," he said, crossing his arms on the table and leaning on them, looking straight into her eyes in a way that made her feel breathless. "Now that you know I'm not a drunk, would you be willing to go out with me?"

His question startled her. She wanted to say yes. She would love to go out with him. In fact, the intensity of her desire startled, even frightened, her a little. She sat back in her chair.

"Oh. Well, uh, I—I don't think that would be such a good idea."

He looked puzzled. "Why?"

She shrugged. "What I told you the other day is still true. I hardly ever date. I don't have the time for it."

He grinned. "Then give me a time limit. I'll set my watch alarm."

She grimaced. "I don't mean it that way."

"What do you mean? I'm lost."

"Oh, you know..." She waggled her hand vaguely. "I have a lot of things to do—the house and the business and my family. They keep me busy and I, well, I have just about all I can handle." He continued to look at her, and she stumbled on, "I'm responsible for my family, you see. Riley and Cathy, even Granddad, in a way. My parents died a few years back."

"I'm sorry."

"Thank you. Anyway, I was the oldest child. The only one who wasn't still a minor, and I couldn't leave all the burden on Granddad."

"That's an awful lot of responsibility for someone as young as you must have been."

She shrugged. "There wasn't anything else to do. I'd always looked after them, anyway. I'd helped out at the store in the summer and after school, so I knew most of what I had to do there, too."

"Still . . . knowing what to do is very different from being responsible for doing it on a permanent basis. It must have been tough for you."

"There were times." Julie smiled at him. He was certainly right about that. And his ready sympathy and obvious admiration for what she had done warmed her.

"No wonder you think I'm idle and useless."

"I didn't say that!" she protested.

He grinned. "You didn't have to."

"Well, all I'm saying is that I have the store to run and the kids' school activities to supervise, the house to keep up, and the animals to feed. That takes all my time and attention."

"Sounds to me like a break is exactly what you need."

"Oh, but dating's not a break. Going out on a date means spending hours trying to decide what to wear and putting on makeup, fixing your hair . . . and then worrying for hours afterward about whether or not he liked you and if he's going to call you again.''

Not to mention all the time she would spend daydreaming and mooning around over Tag, which she wasn't about to reveal to him. There was no way she could explain that going out with him would not be an ordinary date. She could see all too clearly how easy it would be to fall in love with Tag, to be left with a broken heart when he moved back home in a few weeks. And a broken heart was something she didn't have the time or energy to deal with.

''You don't have to worry about what you wear or make a big production out of it. Go as you are.''

''Like this?'' Julie cast an expressive look down at her well-worn shirt and jeans. She didn't have a bit of makeup, not even lipstick, and her hair was just hanging. ''Puh-lease.''

''You look fine to me.''

Julie glanced up at him, and the sarcastic remark she'd been about to make died on her lips. Tag was looking at her in a way that made all thoughts go out of her head. All she could think of was him kissing her.

She rubbed her suddenly sweaty palms down the sides of her legs. This was crazy. There was no reason to go all melting and juvenile inside just because Tag Marshall had looked at her with sexy eyes. She took a breath to speak but could think of nothing to say. For a moment they simply looked at each other.

Finally Tag said, ''Look, you don't need to decide right now about going out with me. Think about it. I'll call you back.'' He rose to his feet.

Julie stood up with him, thinking that she ought to tell him not to bother to call. But she didn't.

She walked him to the front porch and held out her hand. "Thank you again for what you did for Jackson."

He took her hand but didn't shake it. Instead he held it, his thumb gently caressing the back of it, and he pulled her a little closer. She looked up at him, surprised. He bent and brushed his lips against hers. Julie stopped breathing. She could smell him, taste him, feel the heat of his body. A hot sizzle of excitement ran through her.

Tag's mouth returned to hers, lingering this time. His lips were warm and firm, pressing against hers. His mouth tasted faintly of coffee. Julie shivered involuntarily and moved forward, reaching up and curling her arms around his neck.

Tag made a noise of satisfaction and wrapped his arms around her, pulling her up into him. His mouth moved over hers in sweet exploration.

Julie clung to him, lost in the moment. Finally he raised his head and released her. Julie, who had gone up on tiptoe, sank back flat on her feet, shaken and speechless.

"Good night, Julie." He bent and kissed her once more, lightly and briefly. "Think about it?"

She nodded, though her benumbed mind had no idea what she was supposed to think about. Tag smiled and trotted down the porch steps, striding across the lawn toward his car. She watched him get in his car and leave, still looking until his taillights disappeared around the curve in the road.

She sighed and sat down on the top step. The night was warm and as soft as black velvet—cold white stars distant and sparkling, the silence broken only by the rustling of leaves and, off in the distance, the barking of a dog. But for once Julie paid no attention to the familiar loveliness of the country evening. She was too wrapped up in the wild bubbling of the emotions within her, the fizz of happy excitement mingled with doubt and uneasiness. What on earth was she getting into? And how in the world could she ever cope with a man like Tag Marshall?

Chapter 4

Jackson recovered despite his age. Julie picked him up at the vet's the next day and took him home, where he lay on the floor looking pitiful and lapping up all the attention and affection Cathy and Julie lavished on him. The veterinarian also returned the stained tuxedo jacket Tag had wrapped around the dog to keep him warm. Julie suspected that the jacket was a lost cause, but she took it to the dry cleaners' anyway to see if they could restore it.

She picked the jacket up on her lunch hour one day the next week and was astonished to find that all the stains had been removed. She decided on impulse to run it out to the Marshall ranch. After all, Granddad was at the store and could run it fine by himself for a while, and she had to return the jacket to Tag sometime. It might as well be now as this evening or the next weekend. She conveniently ignored the fact that Mike Kubiak came into the store at least once a week and she could easily have waited and sent it to Tag with him.

Julie turned into the wide gates of the B & K Cattle Company and drove up the smooth asphalt driveway, passing Mike's small house, then the main barn, stable, and corrals, to get to the ranch house. The main house sat on a rise, with a commanding view of the countryside. It was a low-slung, sprawling mansion built of brown brick. Julie had never been inside it, but it looked huge from the outside. It seemed absurd to think of Tag living in the gigantic house all by himself. But then, of course, his friends were here visiting him. He wasn't alone.

Julie stomped on the brakes and came to a rocking halt at that thought. She had forgotten about Marilyn and Kevin and Lane, the two men who were visiting from North Carolina. She glanced at the house. Maybe she should turn around and leave. She could always drop the jacket off at Mike's on the way out, and Tag could pick it up there.

But she was already in front of the house, and if anyone was watching out the window, she would look foolish turning tail and running away. Besides, she was no coward. She wasn't about to admit that she was intimidated by some polished, designer-gowned woman. Taking a deep breath, she turned off the ignition and climbed out of the truck. She was grateful, at least, that she was in the good pickup, not the old black rattletrap.

It was some time before the door was answered. Julie was about to turn away, thinking no one was at home, when the door opened. Tag stood framed in the doorway, wearing next to nothing.

In the first flash of recognition, Julie was aware only of a great deal of tanned skin, roughened by curling black hair. Her mind froze. Her lungs stopped. Then she realized that the narrow strip of dark blue cloth across Tag's flat abdomen was a bathing suit, and that his hair was wet, his body dotted with droplets of water. She blushed at her initial, panicky thought that he was naked, which indicated just where her thoughts tended to wander when it came to Tag Marshall.

"Oh," she said stupidly. "I, uh, thought you weren't here."

"It took me a long time to get to the door. I was out at the pool." Tag smiled at her and stepped back. "Come in."

Julie followed him into the entryway, trying to look as though she didn't feel awkward and embarrassed standing beside him in his nearly naked state. "I brought back your jacket." She extended the plastic-draped hanger.

He took it, looking faintly puzzled. "My—oh." His face cleared. "The tuxedo. Well, thanks. I figured it was a dead loss. You didn't need to get it cleaned." Again he grinned. "But I'm glad you did, if it brought you out here to see me." He reached out and took her hand, linking their fingers. "Come on. Why don't you come out by the pool and sit for a while? The weather's gorgeous."

Julie hesitated. "Well, I really need to get back to the store."

"Surely you can stay for a few minutes." He was gently leading her down the hall toward the rear of the house as he spoke. "Somebody's taking care of the store for you, aren't they?"

"Yeah. Granddad's there."

"See? He can handle it for a while. Have a drink and relax for a few minutes. The housekeeper made some lemonade before she left. The real thing, too. Or we have soft drinks. Beer." They reached the kitchen, and he went to the refrigerator, opening the door. "Let's see..."

"Lemonade would be wonderful," Julie said, forestalling a further search. "Are your friends still here?" she asked casually as he poured her a glass of lemonade.

"No." He put the pitcher back into the refrigerator and turned to open the patio door. "Pool's this way. They left Sunday. Marilyn wasn't speaking to me." He grinned, apparently less than upset by the situation.

"I'm sorry."

"Don't be. I came out here to be alone. Think some things through. The last thing I wanted was to have a country club reunion here."

The stepped out onto the patio. The swimming pool shimmered in the sun. Tag walked to a small table beside a lounge chair and set the glass down upon it. A couple of magazines and a half-empty glass of lemonade already sat there. Tag drew up another lounger for Julie, and they sat down.

Julie glanced at the magazines. *Progressive Farmer. Farm and Ranch.* She cocked a skeptical eyebrow at Tag. "That's what you're reading?"

He chuckled. "Yeah. Hard to believe, huh? I'm trying to figure out something about this business. But I still don't know what half the terms in here mean. Like what's a 'calf creep pellet'?" He touched an ad in an opened magazine. "Something to shoot at calves that aren't cute or what?"

Julie laughed. "Interesting theory. No. Pellets are feed, and you put them in what's called a creep feeder."

"I need you around to explain it to me, obviously. You should stay here. I'd learn a lot."

"Oh, no. There's lots of stuff in there I don't know. I'm no expert in raising cattle. I just know something about feeds."

"You raise cattle, don't you? I thought I saw some in the pasture behind your house."

"We have a few head. And Cathy has a show steer. We have a couple of horses, too. But that's about it. We're no full-scale operation. Certainly not like this one."

"It's kind of an intriguing business," Tag admitted. "Mike took me around the place on horseback the other morning. I'm sure he thinks I'm a big nuisance, but I learned a lot. Did you know that you need about five acres per cow? That seems incredible to me."

"It takes more out in West Texas."

"Yeah, I guess it would. Dryer, less vegetation." He paused. "I know horses better than cows. Maybe I ought to suggest to Dad that we raise horses here, too." He grimaced. "On second thought, that would be a sure way to keep horses off this place forever."

"Do you and your father really get along that badly?" Julie asked curiously. It was hard for her to imagine. She had always been close to both her parents. Though she had argued with them at times like any normal teenager, in general they had gotten along well, and she had never felt that they dismissed her ideas simply because they were hers.

Tag shrugged. "Sometimes it feels like we do. I'm not like my brothers or him. He doesn't understand me. He may argue with Adam or James, but he understands them. They're all part of the great fraternity of attorneys-at-law. The things I do, the things I like, seem petty and inconsequential to him. They're hobbies, things you do in your spare time. And a Marshall should never have any spare time.'' He shook his head and sighed. ''Stupid, isn't it, for a grown man to still be arguing with his father? You'd think one of us would have shut up by now.''

''Well, you could hardly expect that of a lawyer,'' Julie joked.

He let out a short laugh. ''I guess you're right. Do you suppose that means I have more of the lawyer in me than I realized?''

''Could be.''

''Heaven forbid.'' He moved his glass in a circular motion, watching the lemonade swirl within it. ''I don't have anything against lawyers except that I don't want to be one. I couldn't stand being cooped up inside an office every day.''

''I wouldn't like that, either.'' Even the store felt like a prison sometimes, especially in the spring and fall, when the air was mellow and warm, scented with life.

He glanced around him. ''Maybe I ought to become a gentleman farmer. No, rancher, I should say.''

''Well, you'd get to be outside a lot.'' She paused, then added drolly, ''In the rain…and the snow…and the summer sun.''

''You paint such an inviting picture.''

Julie smiled. ''The voice of experience.''

They sat quietly for a while, enjoying the warmth of the sun and the sparkle of the water. Birds chattered in the trees beyond the house, and from far away in the distance, Julie could hear the lowing of a cow. She leaned back against the inclined seat and closed her eyes, savoring the moment of relaxation.

The next thing she knew there was a splash of water, and her eyelids fluttered open. She blinked, trying to pull her wits together. She must have fallen asleep. She sat up straight and looked around. The sun was no longer straight overhead. The chair beside her was empty. Then she glanced at the pool and saw Tag swimming toward her. He came over to the side of the pool and crossed his arms on the rim.

"Hi. Sorry if I woke you up. I was trying to be quiet."

Julie felt embarrassed. "I'm sorry. I can't believe I conked out like that. Why didn't you wake me?"

Tag shrugged. "Why? You looked so peaceful. I figured you probably needed a nap."

She pushed her hands through her hair, rubbing her scalp. She was always groggy after sleeping in the daytime.

"Why don't you come in for a dip?" Tag asked from the pool.

She glanced down at her jeans and shirt. "In this? I didn't bring a swimsuit."

"There are some extras in the pool house. I'm sure you can find one that'll fit."

The water did look inviting. Her skin was hot from sleeping in the sun, and she thought of slipping into the cool water, feeling it envelop her, floating on its buoyancy. "No," she said reluctantly, pulling her gaze away from the pool. "I can't. I have to get back to the store."

"Can't your grandfather run it for one afternoon? Why, he might even enjoy having it to himself for a while."

Julie hesitated. Of course Granddad could run it for an afternoon. He'd often done it when she had to take one of the kids somewhere or go up to their school for some reason. Why, he'd helped out at the store long before she ever started working there. Just because she would be taking off time for fun instead of responsibility didn't alter the fact that the store wouldn't suffer. But it stirred up guilt inside her to think of shirking her duty in order to just do nothing.

"Come on," Tag wheedled, seeing her hesitation. "You'll enjoy it. And it'll be good for you—get rid of your stress. You'll feel a hundred percent better."

"I don't know." It seemed wrong, somehow, to dump her responsibilities just for an afternoon of swimming with Tag. "What if there's too much business for Granddad to handle? Or if Riley or Cathy need me at school?"

"Is there usually that much business at this time of year?"

"No," she admitted slowly. "It's the slowest, next to summer. People have just cut their hay, and the cows can eat off the pasture. We don't sell a lot of feed. There's no planting." And the likelihood of Cathy or Riley needing her at school was remote.

"Then?"

"Then…maybe I could stay…for a little while. But I should get back by 5:30, so I can help Granddad close up."

Tag grinned. "That's the pool house over there. Check in the chest by the door—that's where the swimsuits are."

There were several swimsuits in her size. Julie chose a modest turquoise one-piece suit and put it on, then twisted her hair up into a knot on top of her head and secured it with several bobby pins from her purse. She found it hard to believe that she was actually doing this. When was the last time she had chucked work to laze away an entire afternoon? She couldn't remember. She didn't think it had been since she was a teenager, back before her parents had died. How had she let Tag talk her into it? Why was it so difficult to resist his coaxing?

Julie didn't want to think about that. She turned and walked out of the pool house. Tag was swimming laps. When she cautiously walked down the steps into the pool, he turned and stroked lazily back to her. He stood up when he reached her, and the water streamed off his body. Her eyes were drawn to his chest and shoulders, slick with water, the black hairs matted to his skin. Muscles contoured his lean body. Julie found she wanted to reach out and smooth her hand over the curves of his arms and chest, to feel the firmness beneath his skin. Unconsciously she linked her hands behind her back, as though to keep herself from doing just that.

"Hi." Tag swept his wet hair back from his face with one hand.

His eyes fell to her chest and Julie realized the way she was standing, hands behind her back, her breasts thrust out. Quickly she dropped her hands down to her sides. "Hi." She crossed her arms across her chest.

"You look nice."

"Thanks." She couldn't stop the shiver that ran through her.

"Cold?"

"A little. The water's cooler than I expected." She wasn't about to tell him that it was less the temperature of the water than the touch of his eyes that had made her shiver.

"Swim a little, and it'll feel great." He stretched out into a sidestroke.

Julie sucked in a breath and followed him. She had to admit it did feel great. She swam up and down the pool, enjoying the purely physical sensation of using her muscles, slicing through the water, feeling it flow over and around her. Then she turned over onto her back and floated, closing her eyes against the sun and letting the water support her. She felt weightless, relaxed, carefree.

Then something grabbed her foot.

She shrieked and came up with a start. Tag was standing at her feet, grinning. "Why, you..." The sudden burst of adrenaline through her body found its release in laughter. "You scared me to death!"

"Sorry." His eyes were dancing, and he looked anything but apologetic.

Julie swept water at him with her palm, and he jumped back, laughing. She started after him, and he began to swim away. Julie swam after him. He made a pretense of evading her, but let her catch up to him. She grabbed his ankle, and suddenly he twisted, coming back around to grasp her waist. He stood up, lifting her above the surface, and she shrieked and laughed, wrapping her arms around his neck to keep him from tossing her into the water. They wrestled and tumbled and played, laughing and yelling like teenagers. They turned and twisted, their bodies slick, their hands sliding over each other.

Then suddenly his arms were around her, pulling her closer to his body, and his skin was hot as fire. His mouth found hers, and excitement shot through her.

The playful teasing had aroused her unconsciously, so that now her body flamed to life. His kiss was hungry as his tongue claimed her mouth. She welcomed his invasion, her own tongue twining around his.

With one arm holding her tightly to him, their lips clinging, Tag moved slowly down the pool, his legs and free arm cutting smoothly, lazily through the water. Julie felt the water move around her body, curling around her legs, gliding over her flesh. Its touch was a caress in itself, cool and subtly arousing. She felt weightless, will-less, excitingly unlike herself.

Tag reached shallow water and stood, lifting Julie up with a strong arm under her hips so that her mouth was on a level with his. She felt the cool touch of the air on her wet shoulders and back, and her breasts tightened in response, the nipples pointing and pressing into his chest. His hand slid over her water-slick body, caressing her back and hips and thighs, then moved around her leg and up between their bodies, finding the pillowy softness of her breast and cupping it. His thumb circled her hardened nipple, and he groaned low in his throat.

Unconsciously Julie raised her legs in the water and wrapped them around him tightly, pressing herself intimately against him, seeking to satisfy the throbbing ache between her legs. His kisses were driving her wild, his fingers on her breast feather soft and maddeningly erotic. She was astonished to hear herself moaning and realized she was rubbing her body against his.

At the sound she made, Tag's lips left hers and trailed hot fire down her throat and chest. He lifted her higher out of the water, and his eyes ran down her body to where the soaked swimsuit outlined the soft curves of her breasts. Her nipples stood out beneath the thin material like hard, tiny buttons, pressing toward him. Under his frankly sexual gaze they hardened even more. Slowly, watching her breasts all the while, he circled one nipple with his forefinger. Gently he rolled it between his finger and thumb, teasing it into a diamond point of desire.

Julie swallowed hard, her eyes closing at the wash of passion that poured through her. She was pulsing and hot, her skin trembling under the onrush of desire. Was this what it was like to truly want someone? She had never experienced such a raw, savage surge of passion before. She wouldn't have thought it possible until now. She found herself wanting to twist and moan, to tighten her legs around him with all her strength.

Her eyes closed, she didn't see Tag bend his head, and when his lips closed around her nipple, she bucked at the unexpected electric shock of pleasure. His lips worried the fleshy bud through the cloth of the swimsuit, using the covering to gently abrade the nipple. He circled the button with his agile tongue, then lashed it with wet, velvet strokes. Julie whimpered, her fingers digging into his shoulders. She felt as if her whole world were whirling and he was her only anchor, as though she might fly apart into bright, swirling sparks at any moment unless she held on tightly to him.

Tag murmured something that might have been either a curse or a prayer, and his hands slid down to her buttocks, digging into them fiercely. "Julie. Ah, Julie."

He released her with one hand and brought it up to the strap of her swimsuit, pulling it down off her shoulder. The neck of the suit rolled down on that side, exposing one creamy, pink-tipped globe.

Tag's eyes darkened as he gazed at her breast, soft and rounded, the peak rosy from the pull of his lips and glistening with moisture. Almost reverently, his hand came up to cup her breast, and his thumb stroked over the nipple. His tanned flesh was dark against the pale skin. Engorged to a dusky pink, the nipple pebbled at his touch. The sight of his hand on her heightened his desire. He felt aching and huge. He longed to rip her suit off and plunge into her right there in the pool, the sun warm on his back and the water rippling around them.

Taggart Marshall had known his share of women, probably more but he'd never before experienced desire this intense, or this sudden and explosive passion. It was astonishing and exciting, yet faintly scary, as well—as if he no longer knew himself and wasn't fully in control of what he did. He had to stop. Julie was not the kind of girl for a quick, heedless romp in the hay. As much as she excited him, he had sensed her inexperience in her touch and her kiss. She was unaccustomed to this sort of thing. And he knew, somehow—as much as he had ever known anything—that she did not consider sex as something separate from love. If they went ahead and made love, she would probably regret what she had done—and she would hate him for leading her into it.

Which was why he ought to pull away from her right now, give them both a chance to cool down. It was frightening to realize that he wasn't sure that he could do that.

Tag bent and brushed his lips against her nipple. He had to taste her just once. But he found just once wasn't enough. His tongue curled around the bud, savoring the texture, the smell, the essence of her flesh.

He kissed the nipple, his fingers pressing lightly into her breast. He pulled it into his mouth, laving it with exquisite care, slowly, gently sucking it.

Julie drew a ragged breath, moaning at the streak of fire that shot through her when his mouth fastened on her flesh. Her breasts felt swollen and achy, but it was an ache that only the touch of his hot, wet mouth could take away. She wanted to feel his mouth all over her. She wanted him to sink into her, to pierce the throbbing center of her desire and vanquish it. She moved against him sensually, aware—and astonished—that she wanted to be naked in his arms, to see his eyes roam her body, feel his hands caress her bare skin. Her hands slid up from his shoulders and threaded through his hair, pressing his head against her. He responded by widening his mouth over her breast and sucking harder. A chord of desire vibrated through her down to her abdomen.

She heard him moan. Felt him quiver. His hand beneath her hips dug into the soft flesh.

"Oh, Julie, no..." He made a choked noise and jerked his head away from her breast, burying it against the tender flesh of her throat. "Help me, or I won't be able to stop."

"Don't," she breathed, lacing her fingers through his hair.

That single word almost undid him. He wanted to sink into her, embed the throbbing ache of his passion deep into her warmth. He clenched his hands and nipped the fleshy curve of her shoulder, fighting to regain some control.

"Don't tempt me." His voice was low and husky. "Or we'll finish this right here."

Just the vibration of his voice sent prickles of heat through her. Julie knew she wanted to tempt him, to break his control, to feel him turning wild and hot and trembling to have her. It was a feeling she had never experienced before, and the very primitiveness of her own desire shocked her. That shocked surprise was enough to jar her out of the haze of passion in which she had been floating. Her brain cleared somewhat, though her body still pulsed with pure physical hunger.

What in the world was she doing?

"Are you sure, really sure, that you want to make love? Here and now?" Tag asked her.

Julie tensed. "No," she admitted shakily.

No, of course she didn't. She wasn't ready. She had never dreamed that this might happen when she had come here today. It was true that she hadn't been able to stop thinking about Tag's kiss the other night, but that was a far cry from draping herself about him wantonly, the top of her swimsuit dragged down to expose her breast, kissing him as if she never wanted to stop.

Hastily she dropped her legs from around him and stood. She fumbled for the strap of her swimsuit and tugged it up, half-turning from him in embarrassment. Reality was rushing back in a hurry now. Julie blushed at the thought of what she had just done. How in the world had she ever let herself get so carried away? She'd never done that before in her life. Tag would probably think it was something she indulged in all the time!

Tag released her reluctantly, his entire body raging at the betrayal of his mind. His hands itched to reach out and pull her back into his arms, and he had to cross his arms over his chest, clamping his hands firmly under his arms to keep them from acting of their own volition. Desire clawed at his gut.

"I'm sorry," Julie said in a low voice.

He saw the red stain on her cheeks, the sparkle of a tear in her eye. "No. Oh, no, don't be sorry." He reached out to her then, taking her shoulders in his hands and turning her to face him fully. He brushed his lips against her mouth, her cheek, her neck. "Please don't say that. There's nothing to be sorry for. I want you. You want me. It's simple. Natural." He smiled and nuzzled her neck. "It's exactly right. At least for me. And if I had thought you were sure..."

Julie pulled away, shaking her head, unable to meet his eyes. "You're right. I wasn't. I'm not." She looked up at him then, her eyes wide with surprise and mute appeal. "I'm not like this usually. I don't—I mean, I haven't—oh, shoot!" She knew she sounded like an inarticulate country bumpkin. Tag would undoubtedly be glad he had recovered his senses in time to stop their impulsive rush toward lovemaking.

She was glad, too, of course. Or at least she was sure she would be once she was able to sort out the tangle of emotions warring within her.

Tag smiled a little and cupped his hand against her cheek. "I know. It's exceedingly...stimulating."

Her eyes widened a little at the open sensuality of his words. His words, the look in his eyes, the sexy grin on his lips, all seemed to be an invitation. Yet he had just stopped their lovemaking. She wasn't sure what he wanted, what he planned. Of course, how could she expect to know what he wanted? She wasn't even sure of what *she* wanted to happen between them.

The passion she had felt with Tag had been over-whelming. Never before had she even come close to the wild, swept-away feeling she had just known. She felt hot and jangling in the aftermath of it. Just standing there looking at Tag, she knew she still wanted him. If he kissed her again she was afraid she would melt. It was exciting. Delightful. She wanted to experience it again.

But she was also convinced that getting involved with Tag Marshall was dangerous, at least to her emotions. He might not be the selfish drunk she had assumed him to be, but nevertheless, he was way out of her league. He was sophisticated. Worldly. He had probably engaged in dozens of love affairs—and with women far more glamorous, beautiful and intelligent than she was.

She, on the other hand, had never had even one af-fair. Oh, she had dated. She'd even gone steady once in high school. But when she'd returned to Brinkman after her parents died, she had dated less and less. There weren't many available men in a small town like this. Most of the boys she had gone to school with had either married or moved away. In any case, she al-ready knew them, and none of them appealed to her. Besides, what with the store, the house and the kids, she had been too busy to date.

Julie didn't know how to have a casual affair. And she doubted that Tag Marshall knew how to have anything else. But a casual affair was all there could ever be between them. He was marking time until he returned home to his country club life. He was inter-ested in her only because there weren't many options in Brinkman. Before long he would decide to go back to North Carolina, or he would receive a summons from his father, and he would pack up and leave. She would be left behind. Heartbroken.

That was precisely why she had been determined not to be seduced by Tag's good looks and easy charm. But somehow he'd sneaked past her defenses, and here she was, right in the mess she had promised herself to avoid.

Julie sighed and moved away. "I'd better be going. Granddad will wonder what's happened to me."

Tag reached out and grabbed her hand, lacing his fingers through hers. "No, wait. Don't go yet." He knew it would be best if she left. With all the unspent passion boiling inside him, it wouldn't be long before he was kissing and caressing her again. It would be better for them to start fresh another day. But he couldn't keep from asking her to stay. He wanted her with him.

She shook her head and tugged against his hand, not looking at him. "I have to go. Really."

Tag didn't release her hand. Instead he began to rub it gently with his thumb. "When can I see you again?"

She cast him an agitated glance. "I don't think that's a good idea."

He raised his eyebrows. "You're not going to tell me after all this that you don't want to be with me."

"It's not that. It's just…well, it's not a good idea."

"That's what you said before. It still doesn't make sense."

"It does to me." She wasn't about to embarrass herself by admitting how vulnerable she was to him.

"Let me convince you otherwise. Go out with me. You'll see. You'll have a good time. I promise."

"I don't want to—" She made a vague gesture toward the water behind them. "—to get involved in anything like this again."

"Then we won't. I promise." He released her hand, raising his in a gesture of innocence and trustworthiness. "We'll go someplace where there are lots of people. How about that?"

She glanced at him uncertainly, beginning to gnaw at her lower lip. She ought to be firm. She ought to say no. She had to take charge of the situation and not let her emotions run away with her. And yet... "Well, okay. As long as it's daytime and a public place."

"Okay. How about a restaurant? We'll drive to Austin."

She thought of the drive alone with him, an hour each way. Maybe nothing like this would happen, but it wouldn't be healthy for either her heart or her resolve to spend that much time alone with Tag.

She shook her head. "Let's do something here."

"Okay." She could see in his eyes that he was wondering what in the world there was to do in this town that would suffice for a date.

She thought of suggesting that they go dancing at the SPJST hall, but decided that spending an evening in Tag's arms was not a good idea, even if it was in the middle of a crowded dance floor. Besides, an evening date was too romantic.

Suddenly her brow cleared, and she grinned. "I know. St. Theresa's is having their annual bazaar this coming Sunday. It's a big deal. People come from miles around just to eat the barbeque beef and sausage and besides the barbeque, there are games and craft booths and stuff. An auction. And bingo, of course."

"Oh, of course." Tag pulled his face into an expression of mock gravity. "We wouldn't want to miss that."

"If you don't want to, we don't have to go," Julie responded blandly.

"Did I say that? I'd love to go. It sounds delightful. What time shall I pick you up?"

"I can meet you there."

He shook his head. "No. You got to choose the place. I get to decide this. I'll pick you up. One o'clock?"

"Okay." She turned and climbed out of the pool quickly, feeling foolish, as if she were running away from Tag. Well, she admitted to herself, that *was* what she was doing. She was afraid that if she lingered any longer he might kiss her again, and then she didn't know what might happen. She had just proved that she couldn't really trust herself where Tag was concerned.

She walked across the patio and into the pool house to change into her clothes, aware the whole time of Tag's eyes on her back. She didn't understand how just knowing that someone was watching her could make her feel so tingly.

Julie suspected that she'd done something very silly by accepting a date with Tag. But silly or not, excitement was already starting to build in her stomach at the thought of seeing him again on Sunday. However dangerous Tag Marshall might be, she knew that she wanted to run straight into that danger.

Chapter 5

On St. Theresa's bazaar Sunday, denominational boundaries were set aside and almost the entire population of Brinkman converged on the lawn and parking lot beside the brown brick Catholic Church. The bazaar was an even bigger draw than a Friday night game against Thorndale, because hundreds of children who had grown up and left the little town for the brighter lights of Austin, Houston, or Dallas returned home for a visit, and outsiders from Austin and other Central Texas towns traveled to Brinkman for a taste of St. Theresa's famed barbeque beef and Polish sausage.

The long row of barbeque pits was presided over by Floyd Muzycka, one of Vicky Kowalski's many great-uncles, who had held the position ever since Julie could remember. His baster of choice was a long-handled rag mop, which he had bought for that purpose at least twenty years before, and which he carried on his shoulder as he strode up and down the row of smoking barbeque pits, stopping now and then to dip it into a wide bowl of sauce and slap it onto the sizzling meat inside the covered metal cookers. Floyd had earned the honor of chief barbequer not because he was a mainstay of St. Theresa's and a third-degree Knight of Columbus, but because he was the owner of Muzycka's Meat Market, which supplied the slabs of brisket and the popular Polish sausages.

This year, as every other, the bazaar was on a hot September Sunday, so most of the booths and the auction area were clustered under the shade of the spreading live oak and pecan trees. Every now and then a shift of the wind brought puffs of barbeque smoke drifting through the booth area, setting up a rash of coughing, but neither the heat nor the smoke seemed to prevent anyone from eating, drinking and spending money on home-canned goods, games, pastries and T-shirts.

The bazaar started immediately after the eleven o'clock Mass ended, so by the time Tag and Julie arrived at one o'clock it was in full swing. Children, dressed in everything from frilly Sunday school dresses and patent leather shoes to shorts and bare feet, played in the St. Theresa's School playground and darted in and out through the crowds playing boisterous games of tag. Picnic tables and every other available place to sit and balance a plate on one's knees were filled with people eating the barbeque dinner for which the bazaar was famous. The large metal building that was the parish hall was stuffed with people waiting in lines to get their food, as well as row after row of folding tables also crammed with people eating. The din inside the huge, one-room building was deafening, as children shrieked and babies cried and everyone else talked.

Julie watched Tag, amused, as he took in the scene. His eyes flicked over the crowded room; then he turned to her and grinned. "Slice of America, huh?"

"Yeah, I guess." She was surprised by his reaction. When she had suggested the bazaar, she had figured that the noise, heat and hordes of people would bother him. After all, he wasn't exactly used to the amusements of the masses or the joys of small town life. Yet from the look on his face, he seemed to like it.

"Come on, let's get some food," he suggested, taking her hand and pulling her into the shortest of the four lines. "This is quite a production, isn't it? Somehow I'd expected it to be smaller and less efficient. 'Course, I sort of thought I'd see Leo G. Carroll or Barry Fitzgerald in Roman collars, standing around talking to the parishioners."

Julie giggled. "I think Father Ojeleski is a far cry from either of them." She nodded her head toward the parish priest—a short, round young man who was sitting at a table, stuffing down brisket and potato salad while a sturdy, black-haired matron at his side talked nonstop. "That's Mrs. Muzycka with him. She's Floyd's wife—Floyd's the one in charge of the barbeque. You wouldn't think she's almost seventy-one, would you? Her hair's still as black as the first time I saw her. Everybody in her family's like that. She's a Kowalski; her sister is Vicky's grandmother."

"Hey, Julie," said a woman walking past on her way out the door. She was followed by a toddler and a man in his twenties with a broad mustache.

He grinned. "Hi, Jule, how you doin'?"

"Fine, Ray, how about you?"

"Can't complain."

The latter phrase, Tag had learned, was a favorite of the people around Brinkman and usually preceded a long list of gripes about the weather, the government and Southwest Conference football.

Four more people stopped to chat with Julie, and at least seven greeted her in passing. One young woman threw herself at Julie with cries of delight and hugged her. "Julie! I can't believe it! It's so wonderful to see you again!"

"Hi, Ellen. How's Houston?"

"It's great. 'Course, you know me, I'm not like you. I love the city. I couldn't wait to get out of Brinkman." She cast an interested glance at Tag.

"Yeah." Julie ignored the hint in the other woman's look. "You still teaching?"

"Oh, yes. Elementary school. What about you? Married? Working?" Her eyes flickered once more toward Tag.

Perversely Julie continued not to notice Ellen's pointed glances. "No. Not married. I'm running the store, as always."

"Of course. I'd forgotten that." With a last, regretful look at Tag, Ellen sighed and said, "Well, I guess I'd better be going now. Nice seeing you again."

"Yeah. See you next year." As the woman disappeared into the crowd, Julie rolled her eyes. "What a phony. She and I were never friends in high school. She just wanted to meet you."

"At least she has good taste." He grinned.

"Puh-lease..."

"Tell me something."

"What?"

"Do you know everyone in this town? It was the same way at that football game."

Julie chuckled. "Just about. Listen, half the people here are Vicky's cousins. She's related to the Muzyckas, the Kowalskis, the Bielamowiczes, the O'Hara's—"

"The O'Haras? Wait a minute."

Her laugh rang out, light and infectious. "I know. I know. They're the ringers in the bunch. They moved into the area thirty or forty years ago. But she really is related to them. Danny O'Hara married one of her aunts. So Bud and Ann are her cousins."

"Bud?"

"Yeah. Dan, Junior. But nobody ever called him that except his grandmother. See, she—"

"Stop. Stop." He raised his hands as if to ward off her words, his face contorted comically. "I can't take any more local folklore, at least not until after I've eaten. I'm too weak."

The line moved quickly, and before long they had their plastic plates piled high with beans, coleslaw, potato salad and the all-important barbequed beef and Polish sausages. Julie led Tag out of the stifling metal barn of a building to a vacant spot at a wooden table beneath a live oak tree. There was already a family sitting there, but they cheerfully greeted Julie and scooted over so she and Tag would have enough room. Julie introduced Tag all around, and they greeted him with equal cheer.

A white-haired man at the end of the picnic table spoke up interestedly. "Your folks own the B and K?"

"Yes, sir."

"I've always wanted to see one of the owners take an interest in the place. It just isn't right to leave land like that, with never even a visit. You can't make a profit that way."

"Now, Dad," said the younger man soothingly. A dark-haired replica of his father, he flashed an apologetic look at Tag. "You know the Kubiaks would never cheat an owner."

"Hell, no. Did I say they would?" The old man looked offended. "Never knew a Kubiak that wasn't honest. 'Cept, of course, that one over close to Little River who—well, that's not to the point. What I'm saying is, nobody can care for your land the same way you do. Now, our land has been in the Chester name since 1882." He pointed a white plastic knife at Tag for emphasis as he spoke. "And there's never been anybody but a Chester running it. Never will be! The thing is, when it's not your own money you're spending you tend to be a little freer with it. See what I mean? You buy more expensive equipment, sell at a lesser price than maybe you'd hold out for if it was your own. That's what I'm talking about. There's too much money spent at that place."

"Dad, it's a show cattle ranch. It's not supposed to make money."

"Now why in the hell would anybody want a ranch that didn't make money? Huh? I never heard of such a thing."

"I think they bought it as a tax write-off," Tag offered, feeling that he needed to say something to appease the old man, who seemed to take it as a personal affront that the B & K had absentee owners.

"Tax write-off!" The old man's snort clearly indicated his opinion of such tomfoolery. "Never heard of such a thing. Another thing I can't understand is all this foolishness about those fancy registered breeds—

Limousins, Charolais." He grimaced. "You can't make any money off any calf that costs three thousand dollars when beef is selling for sixty-five cents a pound in the market.

"You breed them," his son explained. "You sell the offspring for the same kind of prices. You don't sell them for meat."

"Yeah, only if you can find some other damn fool who'll pay that much to have a cow he can only look at."

Julie glanced at Tag a little nervously, wondering how he was taking the querulous old man's attack on his family's ranching operation. She was relieved to see that he was grinning, his eyes alight with interest and amusement.

"You have a point there," Tag admitted.

"'Course I do." The old man thudded his fist down on the table for emphasis, glad to have an audience that recognized the correctness of his viewpoint. Thus encouraged, he went on to expound at some length upon his opinions regarding ranching and farming.

Julie breathed a sigh of relief when the Chester family finally persuaded the grandfather that it was time to end his discourse and leave the picnic table. "Thank heavens. I could see him getting ready to launch into a monologue about farming during the Depression."

Tag chuckled. "He was harmless. He was rather interesting, actually. I enjoyed listening to him."

Julie realized that he really *had* enjoyed it. That was what was so amazing—Tag seemed to have fun the whole afternoon. He plunged into the simple pleasures of the bazaar with no hint of condescension. He wandered through the arts-and-crafts and game booths, hand-in-hand with Julie, stopping to toss a few sets of softballs at wooden milk bottles and win her several gaudy trinkets or to purchase a cake at the baked goods booth of St. Mary's Society of Church Women. They even went into the perish hall after the lunch had been cleaned up and sat in on a round or two of bingo.

Later, as they strolled out of the parish hall and across to the large tent where the auction was to be held, Julie looked up at Tag and smiled, shaking her head. "I can't believe this. I would never have figured you'd stick it out this long."

His eyebrows rose lazily.

It was an expression that Julie found was growing more and more endearing to her.

"Why not?"

"I figured you would get bored. I thought you'd find it a bit too rustic and simple."

He shrugged and grinned. "I believe in experimentation. I'm not nearly as narrow-minded as you think."

"I didn't mean that."

"No? Then why wouldn't I enjoy it? It's fun. I'm with you. I get to talk to people and enjoy the outdoors. What's not to like?"

"When you put it like that . . . nothing, I guess."

"You, Miss Farrell," Tag tapped her lightly on the end of her nose, "have a bad case of Small Town Defensive Attitude. Has anyone ever told you that?"

"No." Julie had to smile at his words. "Not really. Is this affliction one you discovered yourself?"

"Yes. I first came upon it whenever I'd visit my Grandmother Taggart when I was a child. She was born and raised a country girl and returned to her home, a speck on the map called Martinville, North Carolina, after her husband died. I used to visit her in the summers, and it didn't take me long to notice that everyone there kept telling me they were sure I was having a boring time. Actually, I had a blast—chasing fireflies in the evening, being able to ride downtown on my bike, going out to Grandmother's family's farm and riding horses. It's the same thing here, except such statements are always mixed in with comments like, 'Bet you never seen a sky like that 'un back there in the city, boy.'" He strung the words out in a semblance of a Texas drawl.

Julie laughed. "I heard that one when I came back from college."

"I had trouble deciding whether they liked the place or hated it. Half the time they were downright jingoistic, and the rest of the time they were telling me how much I must dislike the place. Finally I realized it's all a part of the same disease."

"Small Town Defensive Attitude."

"Right. Everybody wants to say that you dislike it before you get a chance to put it down. It's a way of saving face. Besides, there's a kind of strange sort of pride in it. You know, like talking about how terrible the weather is. I have never been anywhere that people didn't think they had the worst weather in all the world—and were just as proud as punch to tell you all about it."

Julie laughed. "You know what? You just might be right."

"Of course I am."

They walked into the shade of the auction tent and found a seat near the rear. A breeze had sprung up as the afternoon had worn on, and it was almost pleasant beneath the awning, as long as they sat near the edge where the breeze could fan them. The auctioneer was another long-time parishioner, Vic Dudek, and though he was not a professional he had a lively, humorous patter that kept the audience awake and the auction moving at a fast pace.

"I didn't expect to see you here," Mike Kubiak said sotto voce to Tag. He had come up in the aisle beside Tag's chair.

Tag glanced at him. "Hi, Mike. Join us?"

Mike's eyes went past Tag to Julie. His mouth tightened, and faint frown lines creased his forehead. Julie knew that seeing her out with Tag was probably a blow to Mike, even though she'd never given him any hope of a relationship with her.

She smiled a little. "Yeah, sure, why don't you?" She scooted down a seat, giving Mike an empty chair on the aisle.

"We still going to the auction tomorrow?" Mike asked Tag.

"Sure, if you've got the time."

"Yeah. No problem."

"What auction?" Julie asked.

"Horses. At a farm down close to the coast. Place went bankrupt and they're auctioning off the stock."

"I was thinking of maybe getting a horse to train," Tag explained.

"Really?"

"Yeah. I've helped train a couple, and I enjoyed it. I've always wanted to try it again, and this seemed like a good opportunity."

Training a horse...didn't that indicate that he would be staying here for a while? Julie tried to suppress the hope that leaped up in her at the thought.

Tag made a purchase and then they decided to leave. He went to the side of the tent to pay for the tack he'd bought, and Julie waited for him with Mike, who glanced at Julie, then followed her gaze to Tag, where he stood smiling and talking with Helen Dudek, the cashier.

"You really like him, don't you?" Mike asked quietly.

Surprised, Julie looked at him. "Tag? Yeah, I like him. Don't you?"

A faint smile touched Mike's lips. "Sure. He's hard not to like. Believe me, I tried. But I don't think I like him the way you do."

Julie sighed. "No. I imagine not."

"He's a nice guy. Real natural. Doesn't put on phony airs or act like he's rolling in dough."

Julie smiled, unaware of how much the glow on her face gave her away. "Yeah. That's true."

"But he won't be staying here forever, you know."

"I know." She looked at Mike and shrugged. "Sometimes logic doesn't make much difference."

He nodded. "Yeah." For a moment they were silent; then Mike said, "Well, I guess I better get on back. Lots of that damn paperwork to do."

"Sure. Goodbye."

He stood up and stepped out into the aisle.

Inspiration hit Julie, and she held out a hand. "Say, wait." She followed him into the aisle, and they walked out of the tent together. "Would you do me a favor?"

"Name it."

"I told Vicky Kowalski I'd send Riley over to help her carry some of the heavy kitchen stuff out to her car. She's working on the cleanup detail in the kitchen.

But I haven't been able to find Riley anywhere." The first part of the story was true, but the second part wasn't. She knew exactly where Riley was. However, he wouldn't mind missing out on a job like this one, and Julie wasn't one to let a golden opportunity for matchmaking slip away. "Do you think you could give her a hand? It won't take long, I promise."

"Sure. I don't mind."

Julie watched as Mike strode off toward the kitchen door at the back of the parish hall, congratulating herself on her skills as a matchmaker.

"What are you looking so pleased about?" Tag asked, coming up behind her.

Julie turned and smiled up at him. "What I hope will be a happy conclusion."

"To what?"

"Some meddling on my part."

Tag glanced in the direction in which she had been gazing and saw Mike's back as he reached the kitchen door and opened it. "Mike and your friend? What's her name? Vicky?"

Julie stared at him. "How did you know?"

"Lucky guess. There was something about the way you were acting at that football game that made me suspect you were trying to throw them together. I take it you just did it again?"

"Yes." Tag took her hand and they began to stroll across the church grounds toward his car. "I'm usually not such a busybody. It's just that in this case... Vicky likes him a lot, and she's my best friend, always has been. And Mike is so obtuse!"

"He may be more aware of her than you think. The other day he was talking about hiring her cousin Tony Something-or-other—"

"Bielamowicz."

"Right. But most of the time when he was talking about Tony, he was actually talking about Vicky—how he'd known her in high school, and what a skinny kid she was then, and how pretty she was now, and what she did for a living, and who her parents are, all that stuff."

"Really?" Julie brightened.

"Really. He's interested in her. 'Course, he may not know it yet."

They reached the car, and Tag glanced across the street. "What's that? The church cemetery?"

"Yeah. You want to walk through it? It's interesting. There are some old tombstones that are written in Polish, the dates and inscriptions and everything."

"Okay."

They crossed the street and wandered through the tombstones. The newer sections were laid out in squared rows, devoid of trees. But in the back of the cemetery the graves were shaded by huge oak and pecan trees and lay in irregular groupings. Many of the stones were encrusted with moss. Some had sunk halfway into the soft ground or had been toppled over. A few of the markers were wooden, all traces of names and dates weathered into nothingness. On others the words had been crudely scratched with a sharp instrument.

"You're right. It *is* fascinating." Tag squatted down to look at the Polish writing on one stone. "This word must be 'born,' and that's probably a month. Five something-or-other—1863. What is this, the name of a town?"

"Yes. Katowice."

"What about your family? I mean, obviously Farrell's not Polish."

"No. We're from the Southern group, the ones who came here from Alabama or East Texas or Mississippi. My parents aren't buried here. They're out at the town cemetery."

They strolled along in silence for a moment; then Tag asked softly. "How did your parents die—I mean, if you don't mind talking about it."

"No. I can talk about it. It was a long time ago. Six years. They were killed in a car wreck. A drunk driver in a pickup ran a stop sign at a highway intersection, and they ran into him. They were returning home from taking me back to college. I'd been here visiting for the weekend."

"It must have been devastating for you."

"Yes." Tears pricked at her eyes even at the memory. "I felt so guilty. You know...if I hadn't been homesick, they wouldn't have brought me home for the weekend, and they wouldn't have been on the highway at that moment."

"And if you hadn't gone away to college you wouldn't have been homesick, and if you hadn't been born none of it would have happened."

"I know. It's not something you should blame yourself for. And I stopped doing that. I got over it. I adjusted. But, oh, it was hard to lose them! We were always so close. I mean, there were a bunch of us kids—five—but every single one of us felt really close to Mom and Dad. They loved us all like only children. They were never too tired or too busy to listen to us or help with any problem. I guess it was weird for a teenager to feel that way, but I knew I could go to my mother with the worst kind of trouble and she would help me. They taught us to be close, to love each other. 'There's never anybody who loves you better than family,' my mother used to say.''

Tag grimaced. ''I guess that's true for some families.''

''Your family isn't close?''

''In some ways. We're loyal to each other, that's a Marshall trait. We get along pretty well, I suppose. At least since we've grown up, Adam and James and I don't fight anymore. Adam's even gone to bat for me with our father quite a few times. I like him. We're friends. James and I—well, we're too different. He doesn't approve of me much, he doesn't approve of anything frivolous. He's a very responsible person...uptight...duty-bound. We don't exactly pal around together.''

''What about your parents?''

''They're rather cool, remote people.'' He thought of his mother, dressed to the nines to go to some committee meeting or another, offering that measured, perfect smile to her young son on the stairs. And of his father, handsome and assured in his three-piece suit, hurrying off to the office every morning with a perfunctory wave to the family left sitting at the breakfast table. ''When I was fourteen I went to prep school in Virginia, so I didn't see them much as a teenager.''

''I can't imagine leaving home at fourteen.''

''It wasn't forever. I spent vacations at home.''

''I know. But I had trouble doing that when I went away to college!'' Julie broke a twig from a bush and began stripping the bark away from it, frowning. ''Our lives are so different.''

"Yeah." He reached out and took her hand, stopping her nervous shredding of the twig. "You think that means we're doomed?"

"I don't know. Doomed to what?"

He shrugged. "Never having anything more than a stroll through a graveyard, I guess." He turned to face her, his usually lighthearted expression suddenly serious. "Are we?"

"I'm not sure," Julie began hesitantly. "Do you think there could be anything more?"

"I'd like to think so. I've always believed that what mattered was what a person was like inside, not whether he called the country club his second home or grew up on a farm—or even whether her father gave her a hug and a kiss when he left her at the dorm after a weekend or a handshake and an 'I want to see those grades improve, young man,' when he put him in the car with the chauffeur to go back to prep school. I guess I'm too much of a romantic to think you fall for a woman because she has the same background you do or knows the same people."

His heavily lashed eyes were mesmerizing. Looking up into them made Julie feel shaky and breathless—and incredibly, sizzlingly alive. "Why *do* you fall for a woman, then?"

"Because when she smiles you feel like you just stepped off a cliff, only you never hit bottom." His eyes flickered to her mouth. "Because when you kiss her you forget your name. And everything else. Because when you look at her you know that if you could just hold on to her, you'd never be lost again."

Julie swayed toward him, her hands moving up to his chest. She couldn't think of anything else but kissing him. Her whole body ached for it. She went up on tiptoe and brushed her lips against his. His hands went to her waist to steady her. When she would have moved away, his mouth sought hers again, unsatisfied with the brief touch of her lips. Julie gave a shaky sigh and wrapped her arms around his neck. His arms went around her tightly, lifting her up into the hard contours of his body as his mouth melded with hers.

Slowly Tag released her, and Julie sank back to earth. They stood for a moment, staring at each other. Tag's chest rose and fell with his rapid breathing, his eyes bright with desire. Julie had the feeling that he was waiting for some look, some word, some gesture from her, so that he could pull her back into his arms again.

This was crazy, she thought. Just the other day she had sworn that there would be nothing physical between them again. She had chosen this time and this place to be with him largely because it would be in public and in the daytime, so there would be less opportunity for them to give in to temptation. She had even made Tag promise that he wouldn't try to kiss her. Yet here they were, in broad daylight—and in the St. Theresa Cemetery, of all places—kissing. And she had been the one who had started it!

For a moment she thought of stepping back into his arms, of offering her lips to him again. She knew that he wouldn't hesitate to take her up on the invitation. She wanted to. She wanted to feel his hands on her, his arms around her, to taste his mouth. In fact, she couldn't think of anything she'd ever wanted quite as much.

But she couldn't afford to lose control. She couldn't toss aside reason and restraint for one night's pleasure. The consequences were too hard, the risk too great. She had had six hard years of training in responsibility, and she used it now. She took a step backward, linking her hands together behind her back and pulled her eyes away from Tag's all-too-powerful gaze.

"I'm sorry. I—that shouldn't have happened. It was my fault."

Tag's mouth tightened. "It wasn't anyone's *fault*. A kiss isn't something you need to lay blame for. It just happened."

"We let it happen. I—I encouraged it. I apologize for placing you in such a difficult situation."

"I've been in worse ones, believe me." He recovered his good humor enough to smile. "Come on, Julie. Lighten up. So we slipped and kissed each other. It's not the end of the world."

"Of course not." A tight smile was the best she could manage. "But I think it's time I went home."

"Whatever you say." He took her hand, and they walked back toward his car. Julie thought she should pull her hand away, but it felt too comfortable with Tag's long, sinewy fingers curling around it. How could one man be so damn sexy, unsettling and reassuring—all at the same time?

The drove to her house in silence. Tag walked her up to the front door and lingered there on the porch, leaning against the doorjamb. Julie found that she didn't want to say good-night, either, and she stood with the door open, fiddling with the knob.

Tag smiled. "I don't want to leave. It's hard to let you go. Did you know that?"

Julie shook her head, pleased, but unwilling to admit it. She felt the same way, but she wasn't about to admit that, either.

"When can I see you again?"

"I don't know." She practically had to bite her tongue to keep from saying, "Anytime you want." What she should say was, "Never."

"How about tomorrow?"

She shook her head, appalled at how reluctant she was to refuse. "I can't. I have to stay late at work tomorrow. Mondays are always busy, and it's the last day of the month, too. I have to close out the books."

"Tuesday then. We'll go to Austin and have dinner. Go to a movie."

"Okay." She hadn't meant to say that, but somehow it had slipped out.

"Good. I'll see you then."

She nodded, and Tag brushed his knuckles down her cheek. Julie thought he was going to kiss her again, and her insides tightened in anticipation. But his hand dropped, and he stepped back, then turned and left, taking the porch steps in a single long stride and loping across the yard to his car.

Julie remained in the doorway, looking after him. He turned at his car and lifted his hand in a wave, then got in and took off. Julie stepped inside and closed the door, leaning back against it. She ought to be tired, but instead she felt jumpy and excited. Tuesday night seemed too far away.

She was afraid she was getting in way over her head. But she couldn't work up even an ounce of regret. However foolish it might be, she knew that going out with Tag was exactly what she wanted to do.

Chapter 6

Julie spent almost two hours getting ready for her date Tuesday night. She rushed home from the store an hour early and jumped into the tub for a quick bath. She washed and styled her hair, splashed herself with some of Jill's old perfume, which she'd left behind in the bathroom, and carefully applied her makeup. She spent the rest of the time trying on almost every dress she had and even a couple of Cathy's. She discarded every one as either too plain, too lacking in style, too dressy or too girlish. She stood in her slip, bra and hose, glaring down at the dresses spread out on her bed. She didn't know how to dress for a date with a man like Tag, she told herself, and even if she knew what would be right, she was sure she didn't own a dress that would fit the bill.

Why was she putting herself through this? she wondered. It was crazy. Frowning, she pulled out a flower-patterned dress in a simple, long-waisted style.

It was her favorite, and since she was certain that everything she owned was wrong, she might as well wear something she liked. Besides, she had a pair of pastel high-heeled sandals that went well with the dress and looked rather sexy, she thought.

She was transferring the contents of her purse into one that went with the sandals when she was distracted by the sound of Cathy shouting outside. Julie went to the window and looked out. Cathy was running up from the pasture as fast as she could, yelling.

"Oh, Lord. What now?" Julie pushed up the window and leaned out. "What's the matter?"

Cathy paused and looked up at her. "The cows are out! On the road! I tried to get them back in, but they just went farther. Three of them are in the ditch or on the road, and Moonie's gone clear over to Mr. Mac-Intyre's pasture."

"I'll get the truck and go after them," Julie called down.

Cathy nodded and ran to the barn. She knew without being told that her job would be to keep the other cattle from escaping, too. Julie ran from the room, grabbing her keys as she went. She didn't stop to think about her hose, her heels, her dress or her date with Tag. Even if she had, she wouldn't have taken the time to change. Livestock on the road was a serious thing. Not only was there the possibility of losing the cows, they could easily cause a wreck. Hitting an object as large as a cow when you were going 55 miles an hour could cause serious injuries to the passengers as well as the car.

"Riley!" she shouted as she ran down the stairs. "Go help Cathy! The cows are out!"

Julie burst out the front door and ran across the yard to the truck just as Tag pulled to a stop in front of her house. He stepped out of his car, a puzzled look on his face. "Julie? What's the matter?"

She jerked open the door to the truck and hopped in. "No time to explain. I'll be back in a minute."

Tag loped across the yard. "Wait, I'll go with you." He jumped into the passenger side of the truck, and Julie took off, rattling across the bumps and ruts of the driveway to the road.

"What's going on?" His voice was filled with concern.

"Some of the cows are out. Cathy's gone down to fix the fence so the rest can't escape, but I have to catch the other four." She glanced at Tag. He looked good enough to take her breath away. But his charcoal-gray, fashionable silk suit was hardly the attire for chasing livestock. "You better stay in the truck."

"Why?"

"Your clothes," she answered succinctly.

"I suppose a dress and heels are just the thing for rounding up stray cows," he retorted, casting an expressive look at Julie's outfit.

"I'm used to it." She stepped on the brake and pulled off onto the shoulder of the road, coming to a halt only yards away from three cows standing peacefully in the ditch, grazing. The animals switched their tails and raised their heads, giving Julie and the truck a brief perusal before they returned to their meal.

Julie flung open the door and jumped down to the ground. Unfortunately, the ground beside the shoulder of the road was muddy, and she immediately sank into mud all the way up the heels of her shoes and over the straps in front. She grimaced.

"You would have to choose the muddiest part of the ditch to stop in!" she grumbled, throwing a baleful glance at the cows, who continued to chew as they regarded her with supreme bovine indifference.

Tag got out on the other side of the truck and came around. "What do we do? Try to chase them back in?"

"Easiest thing is to lure them with some range cubes." Julie opened a bag in the back of the truck and pulled out several large brown chunks.

"What is that? Compressed cardboard?"

"No. Cattle feed. They're called range cubes, and the cattle love them." She held them out in her hands toward the cows. "Look what I have, girls. Come on."

The animals' interest was piqued, and they lumbered along the ditch toward Julie. She walked backwards to the hole in the fence, where several interested cows now stood contemplating the flimsy barricade of a tree branch that Cathy had hastily thrown in front of the downed barbed wire. At the smell of range cubes, they pressed forward and shoved past the branch into the ditch, too.

"Oh, great," Julie muttered.

Tag stuck his hands in the bag and grabbed a couple of handfuls of cubes, which he waved enticingly under the noses of the new arrivals. Then he walked into the pasture, the cows following, with Julie and her three strays right behind him.

"Now what do I do?" he called to Julie as the big animals crowded around him. One of the cows butted his hand impatiently.

"Just open your palms and they'll take the cubes," she instructed as she demonstrated. "Don't worry. They won't bite you."

Tag grimaced at her. "I'm not entirely stupid." He had been around horses too much to be concerned about feeding the animals from his hands.

The cows lipped up the cubes and chewed, then came back for more. "Sorry, girls, that's the end," he told them and laughed when one of the cows nudged him in the back, snuffling around him for the scent of more cubes.

"Come on out or they'll drive you crazy," Julie told him, laughing and retreating through the fence.

Tag followed her. Cathy and Riley came over the rise, carrying several boards and a hammer and nails.

"We'll keep them in," Cathy called. She and Riley grinned at the sight of the other two standing in the pasture in their dressy clothes. "Ya'll get Moonie. She's probably eaten up half of Mr. MacIntyre's crop by now."

"She's right." Julie left the fence to Cathy and Riley and walked back to the truck. Her sandals were thoroughly mud-caked by now, and she'd ripped her hose going through the fence. She looked at Tag. His shoes didn't look any better than hers, and the hems of his trouser legs were smeared with mud.

She climbed up onto the bed of the truck and looked across the road, shading her eyes against the glare of the setting sun. Sure enough, there was Moonie, yanking up cotton plants and chewing away. Julie sighed, grabbed a few range cubes and started across the road. Tag followed suit.

She walked down the row, holding out her hands, calling softly to the Hereford. The cow watched her, chomping away at the cotton plant trailing from either side of her mouth. Moonie had obviously decided that the forbidden plants were tastier than the cubes.

"You dumb cow!" Julie muttered, exasperated. "Well, there's nothing for it but to drive her back across the road. Come on."

She walked past the cow and stationed herself and Tag on either side of the animal. Julie clapped. She shouted. The cow continued to eat. Tag joined in the noise. The cow placidly chomped on. Julie slapped the animal on the flank and Moonie shifted two or three steps.

They yelled. They jumped. They waved their arms. They shoved. Moonie regarded them with her absurdly long-lashed eyes and continued to eat. Tag, who had grown hot, pulled off his suit jacket and slung it over his shoulder. At his movement the cow jumped and bolted away—at a right angle to the way they wanted her to go.

Tag and Julie looked at each other, startled, and then took off after her. They chased her around and around the field, leaping rows of cotton plants, yelling and flailing their arms to try to turn the cow in the right direction. Tag twirled his suit jacket in the air. He waved it at her. He dangled it in front of Moonie like some crazed toreador. Cathy and Riley, having shored up the fence, came across the road to help, but neither of them could stop laughing long enough to do much good. They bent over double, clutching their sides and hooting, as they watched Julie and Tag dash about after the clumsy cow—whistling and calling, Tag whipping his Italian silk jacket around, and Julie flapping her wide skirt.

At last Moonie turned her back on them all and, with an air of utter disdain, trotted across the road and back to the gap in the fence. Cathy and Riley pulled aside their makeshift barricade of boards, and the cow trotted through, swishing her tail. Tag and Julie slumped down onto the open bed of the truck, panting, while the teenagers nailed the boards to the fence posts to prevent another breakout.

Tag looked down at himself. His shoes were caked with dirt, and his trousers were liberally spotted with mud flecks thrown up by Moonie's hooves. His shirt, once crisp and white, was also dotted with mud, wet with sweat and smeared with a long streak of green from a plant he had fallen into. He looked at Julie. Her sandals were ruined, one of them missing a heel. Her hose were in shreds, and the hem of her skirt was splattered with mud. One cheek was stained with dirt, and her damp hair was kinking and curling all around her face.

"Which one of us do you think looks worse?" he asked, grinning.

Julie groaned. "Oh...we can't go anywhere in these clothes now!"

"True."

"I'm sorry." She felt thoroughly deflated. After spending all that time getting ready, after all the anticipation of the last two days—and now their date lay in shambles. "I've ruined your evening."

"Are you kidding?" Tag chuckled. "I had more fun tonight than I've had in ages."

Julie shot him a skeptical look.

"It's true!" he protested. "It was just like being a kid again—running and yelling and slopping around in the mud. Besides, it was funny." He laughed a little, thinking of the way Julie had looked chasing the cow.

A giggle escaped from Julie's throat, too. "You did look like some kind of demented bullfighter out there."

They dissolved into helpless laughter.

They wound up going to the Kustard Korner in Brinkman to eat after they washed and brushed the worst of the dirt from their clothes. Cathy and Riley went with them, and they sat in a booth, eating cheeseburgers and laughing as they discussed the "round up" of Moonie.

"How'd you come up with a name like Moonie for a cow?" Tag asked. "Somehow it doesn't seem very Texas farmer-ish to name your cattle, anyway."

Julie rolled her eyes. "We don't name most of them. Although, actually, we have so few we *can* recognize each one. But when Moonie was a calf she was practically Cathy's pet. That was when Cath first got so interested in animals. She—the calf, not Cathy—was so goofy-acting we started calling her Loonie, and then Loonie-Moonie, and eventually it just evolved into Moonie. She has very distinctive markings. It's always easy to spot her. So we continue to call her by name."

"She's still goofy, too," Riley added, stretching his long legs into the aisle and leaning back against the seat.

"I noticed that."

Riley grinned. "Boy, you two were a sight out there. I coulda charged admission."

"You hush," Julie said, smiling at him affectionately. Riley had a special place in her heart. She had been eight when he was born, just the right age to be a "little mother" to him. He had always been a little different from the other Farrells, quiet and dreamy, and she had been sure that he was somehow special. Six years ago, when her parents died, Riley had been the one who seemed the most affected by it, waking at night from bad dreams, cutting classes, displaying sudden bursts of anger, or closing himself in his room and crying. Julie had known that he, more than any of the others, needed some extra love, and she had given it to him, patiently outlasting his storms and holding him when he woke up terrified. Though he was still a quiet boy, still different, he had made it through his pain and had been coming out of his shell the last couple of years.

He seemed to like Tag. Perhaps it was because Riley recognized in him someone else who was different, who didn't fit in with the norm of Brinkman, Texas. Or maybe it was simply because he was from outside the town. If there was one thing Riley wanted, it was to get away from Brinkman. Whatever the reason, Julie was glad he liked Tag—though she wasn't about to analyze the reasons for *that*.

Cathy liked him, too. She giggled at his jokes and traded quips and barbs with him as if she had known him for years. Of course, there was nothing remarkable in that. Julie had yet to see a woman Tag Marshall couldn't charm—from the giggling schoolgirls behind the counter here at the Kustard Korner to the sour-faced old woman who ran the convenience store on the highway. It wasn't just that he was so handsome he could stop a parade. He was eminently likable—easygoing, always ready with a grin or a clever remark, never dismayed at the prospect of trying something new. Tag genuinely liked people, no matter what their age or disposition, and people responded to that. He also enjoyed life, no matter what came along. Who else would have turned a ruined date like this evening's into something fun?

Tag glanced at Julie and found her studying him. He smiled. "What is it?"

She shook her head. "Nothing. I was thinking how well you get along with people."

He snorted. "It's a question of survival. You have to get along when you've spent your entire life with a bunch of trial lawyers' egos."

"Oh, come on, I can't believe your family's that bad."

He grinned. "Maybe not. But they're no shrinking violets, either."

"Somehow I suspect that you can hold your own."

"Are you saying that I have a big ego?"

"A healthy one."

"Healthy? Does that mean I'm vain?"

"It means you're just right." Heat rose in her throat as she realized how much her statement gave her away.

His smile this time was slow and lazy. Sexy. "I could say the same about you."

Her heart began to thud, heavy and fast. Julie didn't know how he could affect her so strongly with only a few words or a look. She glanced away quickly and began to pleat her napkin. Across the table, Cathy was rattling on about one of her teachers, but Julie didn't pay any attention to what she was saying. At the moment her sister's concerns were the furthest thing from her mind.

They left soon afterwards and returned to the farm. Tag came inside with them. Riley immediately retreated to his room, telling Julie he would see her in the morning. Cathy was inclined to stay and talk, but Julie reminded her of the mountains of homework she had been complaining about that afternoon. Reluctantly, Cathy went upstairs, taking a large soft drink and a bag of chips to sustain her through her ordeal.

"You'd never think she could eat another thing after that meal she put away," Julie commented, watching Cathy walk past the den door with her supplies. "That girl could eat the *world* and never gain any weight." She sighed. "'Course, I guess I could, too, when I was young."

"When you were young!" Tag hooted. "Oh, sure. You're such a relic now." He grabbed her hand and pulled her down onto the couch with him, turning so that their legs were stretched out on the cushions and her back was snuggled against his chest. He wrapped his arms around her from behind and rested his cheek against her hair. "Mmm. Your hair smells delicious."

Julie grinned. "Apricot shampoo."

"I've always loved apricots." He nuzzled her ear, then moved down to her neck. His breath was warm against the sensitive flesh of her throat, and it tickled in a way that sent bright, shivery darts of pleasure all through her.

Tag kissed the juncture of her neck and shoulder. His hand moved across her stomach, gently rubbing, and heat flooded her abdomen. She let her head fall to the side, exposing more of her neck to him, and he responded with slow, searing kisses all the way up to her jaw and back down. By the time his mouth reached her shoulder again Julie was trembling. She turned to him, breathless, and his lips met hers.

"Julie!" Cathy clomped down the stairs. "Have you seen my geometry book?"

Julie jumped out of Tag's arms and to her feet. "Uh, no," she called in a shaky voice, smoothing her hair and clothes. She glanced around the room for the book.

Cathy appeared in the doorway. "I can't find it anywhere."

"Have you tried the kitchen?"

Cathy shook her head and walked off. Julie turned back to Tag self-consciously. She wondered if he was used to girls melting whenever he kissed them, the way she did. Probably.

A minute later Cathy tromped back past the den, book in hand. "Thanks!" she called to Julie, waggling the book in their direction. "See you in the morning."

Julie nodded and smiled, then sank down on the couch. She tried to think of something to say, but the only thing on her mind was what they had been doing before Cathy interrupted. "I'm sorry."

"That's okay. I remember where we were." Tag took her by the shoulders and pulled her down on top of him. She was stretched full-length against him, and she could feel the hard bone and muscle of his body pressing into her softer curves. He wrapped his arms around her, and one hand went up to cup the nape of her neck and guide her head down to his. His lips touched her mouth, then returned for a deeper kiss.

His tongue gently explored her mouth. Julie dug her fingertips into his upper arms, holding on to him as the wild, unfamiliar sensations swept through her. His scent, his taste, were intoxicating. As he kissed her again and again, she could feel nothing but him, think of nothing but him. She wanted to touch the bare skin of his chest, to slide her fingers inside his shirt and explore his flesh. She wanted to kiss him forever. But at the same time she wanted to have his lips leave hers and travel down to the soft flesh of her breasts, to feel his mouth on the hardening tips once more. Her breasts grew achy and swollen, yearning for the touch of his hands and mouth. She moaned, lost in the urgency and frustration of her racing desires.

Tag rolled over onto his side, keeping her body tightly against his, and his knee slid between her legs. Slowly his leg moved up and down between hers, sparking a heat that darted up into her abdomen and exploded there. His hands strayed downward to curve over her hips. He caressed her hips and thighs and bunched her skirt in his hand, shoving it upward. His hand crept under the material and up her thigh. Touching the tender flesh at the back of her thigh, his fingers moved up to the curve of her buttocks. Lightly he skimmed across her hip and down to the crevice between her legs. His mouth devoured hers as his hand explored. Julie slid her top leg up over his, giving his hand freer access in an unspoken, but unmistakable invitation.

He groaned, and his lips dug into hers, his breath searing her cheek. He tore his mouth from hers and tasted her cheek and neck in quick, hard kisses, moving downward to her chest. The top of her dress impeded his progress, and he made a noise of frustration. He had to pull his hand away from the damp, enticing silk between her legs to unzip her dress. The zipper stuck, and he cursed softly. He would have liked to simply rip it downward, breaking it, but he forced himself to work it free.

Julie kissed his neck as he struggled with her zipper, and the touch of her soft lips on his skin didn't make it any easier for him to keep a steady hand. At last the zipper slid downward smoothly, and the back of her dress fell to the sides. Tag laid his hand upon the warm, smooth skin of Julie's back. She was so silken and desirable that he was almost trembling in his hunger and his need.

"God, I want you," he murmured thickly, his hand roaming over her back and moving around to the front. He cupped one breast, covered by a layer of silk and lace, and just the feel of it, just the thought of it, made him almost explode with passion. "Julie, Julie." He pulled the bodice of her dress downward so that he could see the trembling globes, swollen and pink-tipped, beneath the fragile containment of lace. The hard buds of her nipples pressed against the delicate tracery, pebbling at the touch of his gaze.

Gently his thumb settled on one nipple. The feel of it through the lace was almost overwhelmingly erotic. He circled the small nub, watching it respond to his touch. He bent and touched it with his tongue, wetting the material. Dampened, the lace clung even more tightly to the nipple. He lowered his mouth to it once more.

The sound of an engine roared up to the house, and headlights reflected briefly through the window, then were shut off. A truck door slammed.

Tag's head snapped up. Julie gasped and scrambled away, struggling to pull her clothes back into place. Her face flamed with embarrassment. How could she have let things get so far when they were right there in the house, with Riley and Cathy upstairs? She raked her fingers through her hair and put her palms to her hot cheeks, trying to will herself back to normalcy.

She glanced at Tag. He had scooted to the far end of the couch, frustration mingling with an errant amusement in his face. "This place is like Grand Central Station," he commented as the front door opened and someone entered, whistling.

There was the sound of boots on the wooden floor, and then Horace appeared in the doorway. "Hi," Julie said unenthusiastically.

"Hi, kids." Her grandfather seemed unaware of the tension in the air as he sauntered into the room.

Julie introduced the two men, and her grandfather shook Tag's hand, then flopped down in an easy chair. "How's it going?"

"Okay," Julie replied. "A few cows got out this evening."

"Did you get them back in?"

"Yeah."

"So that's what you did on your date?" Horace chuckled at the thought.

"We went out to eat at the Kustard Korner."

Her grandfather's amusement grew. "Boy, Jule, you sure know how to show a fella a good time, don't you?"

"Granddad, please..."

Horace hooted. "I guess it must not have been too bad, since you're still here, right, son?"

"No, it wasn't bad at all." Tag glanced at Julie, and heat began to rise in her face again.

Horace looked from one to the other, then stood up and said, "I reckon I better get on up to bed. Nice meeting you..." He nodded to Tag.

"Nice to meet you, sir." Tag rose to shake his hand.

Horace left the room, shaking his head and grinning.

Julie and Tag looked at each other uncertainly. "I...it is getting rather late," Julie began, though they both knew it was only ten o'clock. "I have to get up early tomorrow morning, and..." Her voice trailed off.

"And it's obvious that this isn't a good time or place."

"I don't know if there is such a thing around this house."

"Let's go to my house."

"Oh, no," Julie protested quickly. Everyone in her family would easily guess where they had gone and why, and that would be absolutely too embarrassing. "Not now."

She could have bitten her tongue for adding that last part. Now Tag would think she was eager to continue their lovemaking another time, that she was even angling for an invitation! She started to explain her words, then decided that it would be better if she just let it rest.

Tag took her hand and brought it to his lips, kissing her palm tenderly. "I don't want it to end."

His words shook Julie. She didn't know how to answer. She felt jumbled and quivery inside, incapable of making any rational statement. It seemed impossible that she could be this eager, this excited, this scared and uncertain. This unfamiliar to herself.

"It's okay. I'm not trying to push." He leaned his head against hers. "But you have to know how much I want you."

Julie nodded. "Me, too. It's just—oh, I'm sure that it would be foolish to go any farther, and I don't know what to do!"

He kissed her forehead. "It's not foolish. How could it be foolish?"

She pulled away, casting him an agonized look. Tag wouldn't understand why it was crazy for her to get involved with him, to fall head-over-heels when there was nowhere for their relationship to go. He was probably used to this kind of affair. She wasn't.

She combed her hair back with her fingers. "I can't explain. It just is."

"Everybody deserves the chance to be foolish at least once in their lives."

Julie smiled faintly. "You're a very persuasive man."

"It's my one skill." He stood up and reached down to take her hands and pull her up. "Look. I'll leave now, and I promise not to bug you about it. Just promise me you'll give us another chance. Say you'll go out with me again."

"All right." She knew she couldn't have said anything else, no matter how much logic might argue against it.

"Good." He bent and kissed her lightly on the lips, then lifted his head and stood looking down at her for a moment, trailing his fingertips down her cheek. The look in his eyes turned Julie's knees to water. "Good night."

Still he lingered, and she thought he might kiss her again, but he turned abruptly, as if pulling himself away, and walked out of the den. She heard the front door close behind him.

Julie drifted upstairs to her room, ignoring the eager questions Cathy pelted at her as she passed her sister's door. She closed her own door behind her and lay down on the bed. Linking her hands behind her head, she gazed up at the ceiling, unable and unwilling to keep the smile off her face.

Chapter 7

Julie lay back on Vicky's couch, her hands clasped behind her head. Vicky was sitting in an easy chair nearby, her feet up on the coffee table, grading a set of multiple choice tests while they talked. It was a scene familiar to them both. In years past it had taken place in either Julie's or Vicky's bedroom, where they had sat on the bed or lain on the floor, the stereo blasting away. But though the scene had changed and they'd grown older, the essentials remained the same. They still came to each other to discuss their problems and share their joys.

Right now Julie was discussing the problem of one Taggart Marshall. "I don't know what to do," she said, sighing, having summed up the major events of their relationship for her friend.

"Why not?" Vicky asked, flipping a test page over. "I don't see where there's a problem. Go out with him again, and *don't go home* afterward. Go to his place."

"That's not what I mean. I know how to arrange being alone with him. I'm just not sure if that's what I want."

"Why on earth not?" Vicky looked at her friend, hands held palms upward in question. "He's gorgeous, unattached, rich, nice. What more do you want?"

"I'm not sure. First of all, I want someone who won't be flying back to North Carolina in a few weeks."

"You don't know how long he'll be here, and you also don't know what might happen in that time. Maybe when he leaves you'll go with him."

"I don't want to go to North Carolina!" Julie sat up, swinging her feet to the floor. "I want to stay right here. Anyway, you know as well as I do how unlikely that is to happen. Tag's only interested in me now because there's a pretty limited supply of women in this town."

"Well, thanks."

Julie made a face at her. "You know what I mean. I'm probably about the only single woman he's talked to here, except for that night at the football game when he met you. And anyone can see that you're only interested in Mike—everyone except Mike, of course."

Vicky smiled. "Did I tell you he called me the other night?"

"Mike? No. Really?"

"Yeah. He helped me at the bazaar Sunday. He carried pots and pans and boxes of stuff out to the car for me, and we talked a long time. Then in the middle of the week he called me."

"What'd he say? Anything interesting?"

"He didn't ask me out, if that's what you mean. But I think he's headed that way. You know the Kubiaks. They're always slow as molasses."

"Vicky, that's great." Julie jumped up to hug her friend. "I just know it's going to work out for you. It has to. You and Mike are right for each other."

"Why are you so sure it's going to work out for us and not for you and Tag?"

"A million reasons. For one thing, we're entirely different. Then there's the matter of him being here only temporarily."

"Maybe he'll get swept away by the charm of Brinkman and decide to stay."

Julie cast her friend a speaking look. "Give me a break. I love the place, but it's not exactly a town that draws people."

"Not necessarily. Tom Casterman, the science teacher, moved here about five years ago. His family wanted to get away from the city."

"It's not the same. Tom Casterman lived in Houston and had to put up with the traffic and crime and all that. Tag Marshall lives in a lovely small city and travels around to beautiful, exciting places. He told me his mother flies to New York City a couple of times a year just to shop for clothes. He's used to things happening, to all kinds of society events—balls and benefits and plays. Lunch at the country club. A vacation house at the beach. A Porsche in his garage. Do you honestly think he'd want to stay in Brinkman?"

Vicky shrugged. "I can't speak for the man any more than I can predict whether the two of you are going to fall in love."

Julie groaned. "Don't even say the words. I think I'm halfway there already."

"You talk as if falling in love would be a terrible thing."

"With him it would be."

"I don't know, Julie. So far you've managed to keep a pretty good distance between yourself and love even without Tag Marshall."

"What are you saying?"

"Just that it seems to me as though you're afraid of a relationship or something."

"I haven't had any room for one in my life, if that's what you mean. I've had the kids to look after. The store. The house. The animals."

"I know. You've been busy. But those 'kids' are all practically grown now. And how necessary is the rest of it? Sometimes I think you use it as an excuse."

Julie glanced at her sharply. "An excuse for what?"

"Not getting close. All the people you're close to are the same ones you were close to before your parents died. Your grandfather, your brothers and sisters. Even me."

Julie frowned at her. "Meaning?"

"I'm not sure. It seems significant, that's all. Like maybe because your parents died, you're scared of loving anybody. I mean, you can't help it with the people you already love, but you can keep it from happening with anybody new."

"Well, thank you, Mrs. Sigmund Freud."

Vicky shrugged. "I don't know. Maybe that's not the way it is. But if not, then why are you so scared of getting involved with an absolutely gorgeous hunk of manhood like Tag Marshall? I mean, most people at least have a few dates with someone before they begin worrying about lifelong commitment."

"If it were someone else, I wouldn't worry about it. But Tag is dangerous to my mental well-being. He's too easy to fall in love with. And falling in love with him would be like heading straight for heartbreak."

Then I'd say the thing to do is not see him anymore," Vicky suggested calmly, turning over another paper.

"I know. But I don't *want* to do that," Julie wailed. "That's my whole problem. It's been over a week since we went out, and he wants to get together again, but I keep putting him off. Only it's terribly hard. I *want* to go out with him. I *want* to go to bed with him." She clutched her hair. "I've been going crazy thinking about him and what we did Saturday."

"Hmm. This sounds encouraging." Vicky looked up from her tests and wiggled her eyebrows comically at Julie. "Maybe there's hope for you yet."

"Oh, Vicky, would you stop it?" Julie grimaced at her friend. "I need serious help here. I don't know what to do! I keep thinking about Tag and remembering...and I get all turned on even thinking about him! Now I know what a teenage boy feels like."

Vicky hooted with laughter. "That *is* bad. You know what I think you should do? Stop being the cautious, responsible, mature Julie Farrell for once. You didn't spend enough time being an incautious, irresponsible teenager like the rest of us did. You need to kick up your heels. It'll be good for you. Just say, 'Damn the consequences!' "

"Full speed ahead," Julie murmured.

"Absolutely. Do something just for fun, just because you want to. I tell you what. Isn't Riley helping out at the B and K this weekend?"

"Yeah. They're vaccinating the calves."

"So's my cousin Tony. What I was thinking is, why don't we drop by there tomorrow? You could take Riley lunch or something. That'd be a good enough excuse."

"Excuse for what?"

"To see Tag, silly. Mike told me he's going to be working with them. Mike says he's always willing to try stuff, even if he doesn't know much. Except horses. Mike was impressed by how much he knows about horses."

"But I don't want to see Tag. I mean, I do, but I shouldn't."

"That's precisely what we're working on. If you want to see him, you ought to go. Let loose a little."

"You make me sound like a real stick-in-the-mud."

"You are, when it comes to men. Come on. Don't you remember what fun it was doing stuff like this? Figuring out a way to see Terry Caswell and flirt with him? Remember that?"

Julie giggled. "Heavens, yes! We must have gone to the Caswells' filling station at least three times a week. Terry must have thought we were crazy."

"Are you kidding? He loved it! Why else did he always come out to help us? So he could flirt with you!"

A smile lingered on Julie's lips as she remembered their antics from their high school days. Then she sighed. "But that was a long time ago, Vicky. We were kids then."

"So? You talk like you're an old lady. You're only twenty-five. You can still have fun. You can think up an excuse to see a guy without having to admit you want to. The advantage is, you can see him and flirt and have a good time without really committing yourself. If we drop by, you can leave whenever you want, and with me and Riley and Tony and Mike and the others, it's not as if you'll be alone with him. It's a safe way of seeing him."

"I guess that's true."

"So let's do it," Vicky urged. "I've been an adult now for three years, and I'm getting tired of it. Come on, say you'll come with me. Think how much it'll help your matchmaking plans for Mike and me."

"I don't have to be along for that."

"It's not the same if I go out there by myself, and you know it. You have to come with me."

"Well...I guess I could go after we close the store."

"When's that?"

"Two on Saturday."

"Fine. They'll love having a snack and a drink in the middle of the afternoon. I'll pick you up at the store. Okay?"

"Okay."

Julie was restless the next morning. All the customers' transactions seemed to drag. She couldn't settle down to any one task. Everyone wanted to talk longer than she wanted to listen. She fidgeted and seized any excuse to leave the store.

She knew why, though she hated to admit it even to herself. She was eager to see Tag, and the morning couldn't pass fast enough for her. It was impossible to keep her mind off him; it had been ever since Vicky suggested this afternoon's outing. She kept thinking about the way he looked. Imagining the crisp black curve of his hair, the line of his jaw, the incredibly blue eyes in which there always lurked a hint of mischief. She remembered what he had worn each time she had seen him, and she couldn't decide what kind of clothes made him look the sexiest. Whatever he wore seemed natural and right, from the tuxedo he'd had on the night they rushed Jackson to the vet to the jeans, sneakers and plain blue shirt he had worn to the bazaar.

She also kept remembering his kisses. His hands on her. The feel of his lean body stretched out against hers on the couch the other night. No one had ever aroused her as Tag did. Just a glance from him was enough to make her insides quiver. All he had to do was touch her or kiss her, and she melted. She couldn't remember ever feeling this way before.

Finally it was time to close the store, and Vicky pulled up outside, waiting for her. Julie hurried through her closing routines, tossed a quick goodbye to her grandfather and ran out the front door. She slid into the front seat beside Vicky.

"Hi." She flipped down the visor to check her hair and lipstick in the mirror on the back.

"Hi." Vicky watched her, amused. "You look just fine."

Julie took a deep breath. "I don't feel it. My stomach's got jumping beans inside it. Isn't it crazy to do something that makes me feel like this?"

"Probably crazier not to. I mean, that's part of what's so wonderful about being in love."

"I'm not in love."

"Well, whatever you're in, then. Heat, maybe?"

Julie looked at her friend and rolled her eyes. Vicky laughed. "I fixed a bunch of sandwiches," Vicky said as they zipped down the highway. "And I brought some soft drinks. I called Tony this morning and told him we might come out and bring them something to eat. He thought it was a great idea."

"He would." It was generally known that Tony loved anything to do with eating.

"He says he's been starving to death ever since Bonnie put him on that low-cholesterol diet. He hasn't had any kielbasa in a month."

"I'm surprised they're still married, then."

Vicky laughed. "You and me both."

They reached the B & K and turned in at the front gate, but instead of heading for the house they took the dirt road that split off toward the barn and pens. The main corral held a bunch of cows and calves. Several men were clustered around one chute. Vicky stopped the car, and she and Julie got out. Mike, standing on the rails on one side of the chute, turned and waved, a grin splitting his face.

"Hey! Vicky. Julie. What're ya'll doing out here?"

"Came to bring Riley some lunch," Vicky replied smoothly.

Julie wasn't capable of answering at the moment. She was too busy looking at Tag. He was one of the men wrestling the calves into place and locking their heads in the bars. It was a hot day and hot work, and he had unbuttoned his shirt down the front, letting it hang outside his jeans. His jeans were old and worn, as were the boots on his feet. On his hands he wore tan leather work gloves. Sweat glistened on his arms and slicked down the hair on his chest. His muscles tightened and pulled as he struggled with the calf, and his face was set in determination. He looked hard and elemental, a natural part of the Western scene. Watching him, a heat that had nothing to do with the weather curled through Julie's abdomen. She had never realized before how sexy the thick, rough work gloves looked on a man's hands, emphasizing the nakedness of his arms above them.

When the calf was locked in, Tag let go and looked up. His eyes met Julie's. He didn't say anything, just looked at her. She couldn't read his expression, and she wasn't sure whether he was angry or pleased to see her. But excitement rose in her, anyway.

He nodded once toward her. "Julie."

"Hello, Tag." She couldn't make anything of his greeting. But he didn't leave the chute to come over to her, and she felt the sickening certainty that he was angry with her. She had put him off too much this last week, and she had lost him. Well, that took care of the decision for her, and she supposed she should be glad of that, but she couldn't find any gladness in her.

Julie glanced at Riley. His face was unreadable beneath the broad-brimmed hat, but she was sure that he wondered what she was doing bringing him lunch. She had never done it before. She felt more and more like a fool. Oh, why had she let Vicky talk her into coming?

Vicky opened the trunk and pulled out a cooler and the bag of sandwiches, setting them on the hood while the men continued to work. "There's plenty here for the rest of you, too," she called.

"Sure thing." Mike grinned over at her. "Let us finish this lot here, and then we can take a break."

At least Mike and Vicky appeared to be working out, Julie thought. She hopped up next to the cooler on the hood of Vicky's car and watched the workers.

Tag was obviously inexperienced and not as quick or as sure as the other men in his movements. But he had caught on to what he was doing, and worked hard and well. It surprised Julie. She would never have figured Taggart Marshall for a man who would be willing to wrestle with a bunch of skittish calves in the hot sun, at least not for long. He was, after all, a city boy, and a wealthy one at that. Unused to any sort of manual labor. And as much as she liked him, she thought he was something of a dilettante. Charming and bright, interested in a lot of things, but by his own admission not given to working hard at anything.

As she watched him, Tag glanced up at her. His eyes flickered down her, almost as if drawn against his will. Then he pulled them away and returned to his work. Julie wondered if she had been wrong about him being angry at her. The look he had just given her was that of a man who was definitely interested. She wished she could see his face clearly, out of the blinding sun and without the concealing hat. She wished she knew what he was thinking. Most of all, she wished she knew what she was doing.

It was impossible to watch Tag work and not feel desire ripple through her. He looked too sexy in boots and jeans. Her eyes were drawn to the wide strip of skin visible between the sides of his opened shirt, to the muscles that bulged in his arms as he pushed and pulled the animals into place. His skin was smooth and slick with sweat. His dampened shirt clung to his back.

Heat built in Julie. Her skin felt intensely alive, aware of every stray brush of the breeze and warm touch of the sun.

The men turned the last calf loose in the pen, then left the chute, walking toward the car. Julie watched Tag angle toward her, stripping off his gloves as he walked. Julie slid off the hood of the car to face him, rubbing the palms of her hands nervously down the sides of her legs.

"Hello, Julie." There was a questioning note in his voice, almost a wariness.

"Hi."

"We're about through here. I'm heading up to the house. Why don't you come with me?"

Julie glanced toward Vicky, who was watching them with interest. "Okay."

They walked past the barn and across the stretch of ground toward the large main house.

"I was surprised to see you here," Tag said, glancing sideways at her.

"I brought Riley lunch," she said, repeating the excuse Vicky had given when they arrived.

"Yeah. I heard." His eyes told her he didn't believe that for one second.

Julie didn't know what to say. She couldn't easily admit that she had come out to see him. But neither could she think of any logical reason for her presence. Silence stretched between them.

Finally Tag said, "I was glad to see you."

"Were you?" she blurted out.

The look he gave her was bland. "Sure. Why wouldn't I be?"

"I don't know. You seemed . . . a little cool."

"I didn't mean to be." They reached the side door of the house, and Tag opened it, standing aside to let her through. He followed her in and closed the door, hanging his hat on the rack beside it. He stopped, looked down at his gloves and folded them with considerable care.

"I was confused." He frowned. "After the other night, I thought I knew where I stood. But you've avoided me all week, making excuse after excuse not to see me. And now here you are, dropping in out of the blue." He looked up at her. "What do you want from me? Where are we going from here?"

"I don't know," Julie replied honestly. "If I did, I wouldn't be so damn wishy-washy."

There was a moment's hesitation, then, unexpectedly, Tag grinned. "That's reassuring." He tossed the gloves onto the counter. "Look, I'm not asking for any guarantees. But I wish you would clue me in to what's going on—including the fact that *you* don't know what's going on."

Julie had to grin back. "Okay. Now you probably know as much as I do."

"Except the reason for your uncertainty. Why are you waffling?"

She shook her head, a blush rising in her cheeks. "I—it's not that I don't want you. I do."

She saw the change in his eyes as the words hit him, the darkening and the sudden intensity, though his face remained calm. "Then what's the problem? Do you think I don't feel the same way? 'Cause, believe me, I do."

"No. I know you want me."

He looked at her, puzzled. "Then what?"

"Maybe it's just that when I'm alone and start thinking about it, I get a little scared."

"Of me?"

"Of everything." Julie gestured vaguely. "It's all new to me. I'm scared of making a mistake. Of getting hurt."

"It's always a bit scary, isn't it? I mean, making yourself vulnerable to another person, risking the hurt. Wouldn't you imagine everyone feels some insecurity?"

"I don't know. I can't imagine you doubting yourself in a relationship. I mean, what girl wouldn't fall all over herself to be with you?"

He smiled. "Well, I can think of one Texas farm girl who has displayed a distinct lack of interest in me."

Julie grimaced. "It wasn't lack of interest. Just prudence."

"Okay. I'll admit women like me. I have money and a face."

"Not to mention modesty."

He shrugged. "What, you want me to pretend I think I'm some kind of wart so I won't look vain? What's the point? It's a quirk of fate, just like having money. I was born into a good-looking bunch of people the same way I was born into money. I look like my father. I look like my brothers. It's pure happenstance. I could have wound up looking like my cousin Keith, who's a real toad. Either way, there's more to me than how I look—or at least I hope there is."

"There is," Julie agreed. "And it's all equally appealing. You're kind and good and a lot of fun..."

Tag grinned and put his hands on her waist, drawing her against him and linking his hands behind her back. "Keep talking. I like this part." He sobered. "All I'm saying is that there's nothing that can keep a person from getting their heart broken. Not looks or money or anything else. It's a risk you take every time. But you still take it, don't you?"

"I never have."

It took a moment for the import of her words to sink in. Then Tag's face changed almost ludicrously. He stared. His hands fell away from her. "What?"

Julie stepped back, crossing her arms defensively. "There's no need to look like that. It's not a crime, you know."

"Of course not. I just can't believe..."

Julie cocked an eyebrow in irritation. "It's not *that* strange. I'm only twenty-five, and, well, I'm choosy. Besides, I've been too busy for dating."

His eyes moved down her body. The stunned look was leaving his eyes, replaced by a darkening arousal. "Julie..." He moved toward her, and she stepped back quickly.

"Just a minute. That wasn't an invitation, you know."

"Don't worry, I'm not going to try anything." He stopped. "Why didn't you tell me? I had no idea. The way you kissed..." His eyes went to her mouth.

Julie pressed her lips together tightly, fighting the impulse to wet them with her tongue. It was crazy that Tag could affect her this way. All he had to do was look at her and her skin was suddenly hot. Her breasts seemed to swell and grow heavy, the tips engorged. She squeezed her legs together, all too aware of the teasing ache that sprang up there.

Tag raised his hand and brushed his knuckles down her cheek. "I swear, I'll go slow. I don't ever want to hurt or frighten you. You know that, don't you?"

Julie nodded, at that moment incapable of speech.

He took her chin between his thumb and forefinger. His fingers felt hot and rough against her skin. She couldn't look away from his piercing blue eyes. "We'll wait as long as you want. I won't push you. You trust me, don't you?"

"Yes." Julie's voice came out far smaller than she would have liked. From the way her insides were trembling she didn't think that they would have to wait long.

"I don't know much about virgins." He smiled slightly. "It's a little out of my range of experience. Once I would have said I wouldn't want to find out. But somehow, with you, I find myself wanting to learn."

Julie's breath rushed painfully in her throat. Her heart was slamming against her chest. Tag was powerfully male. Intoxicatingly male. Everything about him practically screamed that any night spent with him would be deliriously exciting, wildly passionate—and utterly without commitment.

Julie took another step back, turning her head away. That wasn't what she wanted. She was insane to even think of getting involved with Tag. She sneaked a glance at him from beneath her eyelashes, and she knew that there was no way she could walk away from him right now.

Tag didn't remark on her backward movement or try to resume the subject they had been discussing. "I desperately need a shower," he said, wiping a sleeve across his grimy face. "Why don't you sit down and wait for me? It won't take long. Then we can do something. How does that sound?"

Gratefully Julie nodded her head. "That sounds fine."

"Okay. Get yourself a drink. Explore the place." He made a vague gesture in the direction of the rest of the house. "I'll be back in a while."

He walked out of the kitchen and down the hallway, peeling off his shirt as he went. Julie watched the play of muscles across his back.

She sat down at the table in the large country kitchen. Her knees felt too weak to go any further. She crossed her arms on the table and rested her head on them. Why couldn't she come to a decision? Why couldn't she come up with an answer? She was going to drive both herself and Tag crazy if she went on like this, blowing hot and cold. Well, no, not cold; she was never cold where Tag was concerned. But she did try to think sensibly instead of letting her emotions pull her along. *Want and should. Desire and reason.*

With a sigh, Julie rose. She had to do something to take her mind off things. She opened the refrigerator and took out a soft drink. The refrigerator was neatly organized, and, unlike hers, the front was bare of notes and lists and letters from school about this or that activity. On its gleaming almond door a single small notepad was held by a magnet, a pencil dangling from it by a chain. The note on top read, "Mr. M—I will not be here Friday afternoon. Will come Saturday morning instead. Mrs. G."

Julie wondered if Tag had seen the note or even been aware of Mrs. G's absence or presence. The house was so big two people could live in it and never see each other.

It was also quiet as a tomb. Julie tried to remember ever being anyplace as quiet, other than a funeral parlor. The store was always filled with noise from the street or customers talking. At home there was always a racket. She supposed there must have been times when she had been completely alone in the house—though she couldn't remember exactly when—but even then there would have been dogs barking or cats meowing.

She wondered if Tag had grown up in a house like this, kept spotlessly clean by servants, quiet and still. She couldn't imagine what that kind of a life would be like. It would be wonderful, in a way, to be taken care of, but it seemed rather lonely, as well.

Julie meandered through the house, aimlessly sticking her head into all the rooms. Each was furnished in a sort of Texan ranch style, all leather and massive wood. She suspected the touch of a decorator, not someone who had ever lived here, and she half-expected to find a pair of longhorns looming from some wall. There were no homey touches. It was almost like a hotel in which Tag was visiting, she thought.

She carefully avoided the bedroom wing, making her way instead to the wing opposite it, where she found a study and a small, cozy den. There were signs of habitation here—running shoes in front of a chair, an open magazine on the coffee table, an empty drink can on the lamp table—and she realized that this must be where Tag spent most of his time. For some reason it pleased her that he chose to relax in this small room instead of the larger, colder rooms in the main part of the house.

She left the den and wandered farther down the hallway. She stepped inside the next doorway and stopped. Her eyes flickered over the room. It was lived in. There were boots lying on their side on the floor and dirty clothes tossed beside them. There were books and magazines lying about, and a shirt thrown over the back of a chair. It was Tag's room. Somehow, despite her best possible effort to avoid it, she had managed to stumble into Tag's bedroom.

Julie knew she ought to leave, but she couldn't keep from lingering for a moment, her eyes once again sweeping the room. She looked at it with more awareness, noticing the things that were Tag's, seeing it as *his* room. It wasn't that there was anything all that special about it. It was only the fact that he lived here, slept here, that made it fascinating to her. She saw the bed and couldn't help thinking of lying on it with Tag, limbs entwined, lost in passion.

She closed her eyes for a moment, envisioning the scene, one hand braced against the doorjamb. Suddenly a door clicked open, startling her. Julie's eyes flew open. She drew in a quick breath. She had waited too long to make her escape. Tag had entered from the bathroom door on the other side and was standing across the room from her, wearing only a pair of jeans.

Chapter 8

Julie drew in her breath sharply. For a moment she was unable to say—or even think—anything coherent. All she could see, all she could think of, was Tag.

He carried a towel in one hand, with which he had been drying his hair, and he lowered it slowly as he gazed back at her. His black hair was wet and tousled, gleaming. A few drops of water lay in tiny beads on his shoulders and chest, glistening against his tanned skin. The bones of his shoulders stood out sharply, in contrast to the smooth, rounded curves of his muscles. Black hairs sprinkled his chest, and Julie followed the line of them down to his flat stomach, where they disappeared into his jeans.

Finally Julie found her voice. "I—I'm sorry." She began to back out of the room and bumped into the doorjamb. A blush spread across her cheeks.

"Don't be sorry." Tag crossed the room toward her. "I don't mind."

"I, uh, didn't mean to come in here. To disturb you."

He grinned. "I rather like the way you disturb me."

"That wasn't what I meant, and you know it." She tried to ignore the way her heart was hammering and the blood rushing through her veins. She had to use her head, not the other, more demanding, parts of her body.

"You're right." The incorrigible grin was still on his face. It was the kind of smile that could make any woman's heart do flip-flops. Unfortunately, Julie thought, she seemed to be even more susceptible to it than most women.

Tag took a step closer, and she quickly backtracked two steps. She could not, absolutely could not, let him kiss her or take her in his arms while they were in the bedroom together. "I'll go back to the living room and wait for you," she said hurriedly.

"Julie, please . . . I don't understand. Don't you know I wouldn't hurt you?"

"It's not you I'm scared of!" she blurted. "It's me!"

"You!" His eyebrows vaulted up. Then understanding washed over his face, and he smiled, pleased amusement twinkling in his eyes. "You mean you can't trust yourself around me?"

Julie scowled. She wished she could call back the words. "Don't get smug about it."

"I'm not." He reached out and brushed his fingertips lightly across her cheekbone. "But I am glad." His hand moved down to the corner of her mouth, and he traced the outline of her lips with his forefinger. His own mouth softened. "I want you to want me. Just like I want you."

Julie felt as if she would melt. Her mouth parted slightly, and his finger moved along the soft inner edge of her lower lip. She could taste the faint salt of his skin, and she knew an urge to run her tongue over his finger, to tease it gently with her teeth. Her eyes closed, and she swayed toward him.

"There's nothing wrong with wanting me, is there?" he went on huskily. "Why do you have to fight it?"

At the moment it was hard to remember why. "I'm afraid," she murmured.

His hand slid down to her throat, fingers spreading wide over the soft skin. "Of what?"

"Falling in love with you."

Her eyes widened as she realized what she had let slip out. She stepped back from him, her surprise snapping her out of the daze of passion. "Oh, no. I didn't—" But there was no way to deny what she had just said.

Tag was watching her, his eyes narrow and intent. "Would that be so horrible? To love me?"

"No. Not at all. It would be..." Feeling flooded through her at the thought of loving Tag. "It would be wonderful."

His face changed subtly, became somehow softer, warmer.

"The problem is afterward, when you leave."

"Who says I'll leave?"

"You're bound to sometime."

"It doesn't mean I'll leave you. What makes you think the feeling's one-sided? What makes you think I'm not falling in love as much as you are?"

"Are you?" She couldn't quell the tremor in her voice.

"I don't know. You've got me turned inside out. Damn it, Julie, I can't go ten minutes without thinking about you. I want you all the time. When I go to bed at night I can't sleep for imagining what it would be like to have you there beside me and wishing that you were. During the day I have to find things to keep me busy, because otherwise I'd mope around thinking about you. I remember every minute that we've spent together. I remember your gestures, your words, your smile. Last week, when you turned me down every time I asked you out, I knew you didn't want to see me anymore. I'm not completely stupid. But I kept calling you anyway, because I couldn't stop myself. I didn't give a damn about pride, or even self-respect. All I cared about was you. I told myself I was an idiot. I was determined to be mad at you. I swore that I'd be cool toward you if I ever saw you again. But the minute you stepped out of that car I went to mush inside.

His words amazed her. She would never have dreamed that the self-possessed Taggart Marshall could have been so disturbed, especially by someone like her. She hadn't even considered that when she turned him down last week she had been hurting him. "Oh, Tag...I'm sorry. I wouldn't have hurt you for the world. I never dreamed that it would cause you pain."

"Lord, Julie, what do you think I am? A mannequin? Do you think I have no feelings? That I'm utterly cold? How can you be afraid you'll fall in love with me when you think so little of me?"

"No!" Julie protested, stung. "I don't think you're unfeeling and cold! It's just that I didn't think you cared enough about me for it to matter one way or the other if I didn't go out with you."

"Not care enough about you!" He looked stunned. "I've been running after you from the minute I arrived in this town, ignoring every rebuff I received from you, coming back for more, time after time—and you think I don't care about you?"

"But you're stuck out here. You have to find something or someone to occupy your time until you can go home. I knew you liked me, that I interested you enough to relieve your boredom, but that's not the same as really being involved with someone. Caring for them."

"Wait just a minute." Tag scowled. "I'm not stuck out here. I chose to be here at the ranch. No one forced me to come. I can go back anytime I want. I just haven't had any desire to. And one of the reasons I haven't is you."

"But your father—I thought he exiled you to Brinkman. Cut off your money or something until you straightened up."

Tag's eyebrows soared. "I'm thirty years old, not some teenage kid whose father controls his life. My father was mad at me, sure. He often is. But he can't cut off my money. It comes from trusts my grandparents and uncle set up years ago. And he sure as hell can't tell me what to do."

"Oh."

"I can't believe this. You not only thought I was cold, you also thought I was so weak and lazy I was willing to let my father control my life because he supported me."

"Tag! You're putting the wrong interpretation on it."

"Oh? Then would you care to tell me what the correct interpretation would be?"

Julie hesitated. Then she sighed. "All right. Yes. I did think you were weak and lazy. There! Now are you satisfied? But I didn't think that because of anything I saw in you. It was because your father told Mike that you were in disgrace. I thought you were being shipped out here until you decided to behave yourself. I assumed you were college age. Then, when I met you and saw that you were older, I figured you must be willing to be controlled by your father and his purse strings. How was I to know any different?"

"You could have judged me for myself, not by what somebody said about me!"

"I did! I liked you. You were funny and fun. Handsome, charming. I enjoyed being around you. I even realized that you were basically a kind, good person. But none of those things excludes your also being a little lazy or weak. Everybody has flaws. I fell for you anyway."

Tag stood looking at her for a moment, then turned and walked away, tossing the towel he'd been holding on the floor. Julie went cold inside. Was he walking away from her forever? Did he hate her for what she had thought about him?

She started after him. "Tag. Wait."

He stopped in the middle of the room and looked back at her. "Maybe you're more right than I like to admit. Maybe I have been lazy and weak. I've gone through my life without a whole hell of a lot of purpose. But, damn it, believe this—I am not the faithless, feckless playboy you think I am. I don't use women then toss them aside, or spend my life in meaningless affairs. I am not incapable of love or commitment or honesty.''

Julie's eyes filled with tears. ''I'm sorry.''

''And I damn sure—'' He bit out each word ''—don't pursue a woman the way I've pursued you simply because I'm bored. I care for you! God help me, I think I'm falling in love with you!''

Julie stared, stunned by his statement.

''You're the one,'' Tag went on, ''who's pushed me away. One day you like me and seem to want me as much as I want you. The next you'll hardly speak to me. I want to know how you feel about me. I want to know where I stand.''

Julie was silent for a moment. ''I—I'm not sure. I want you. Sometimes I want you so much I can hardly stand it.'' She heard the quick intake of his breath and knew her words had affected him. ''And I like you so much it scares me.'' She held out her hands in a sort of mute supplication. ''But I don't want to get hurt.''

He came back to her in quick strides and took her hands in his. His gaze was earnest and intent, and he held her hands tightly. ''I would never hurt you.'' He raised one of her hands to his lips and gently kissed her palm. ''I'd do anything to keep you from being hurt. I can't promise that either one of us will come out of this unscathed. I'm no fortune-teller—I don't know what will happen. But, sweetheart, you have to take a chance sometimes. Otherwise you always wind up with nothing.''

Julie reached up and cupped his cheek with her hand. The feel of his skin beneath hers sent tingles through her. She couldn't remember ever wanting so much to believe someone. She wanted to step into his arms and forget the future, forget the rest of the world. She didn't know if what she felt was desire or love or insanity. But she knew that she wanted to give herself up to it. "Taggart," she murmured, trailing her fingers across his cheek.

He covered her hand with his own, squeezing it tightly against his flesh, and his eyes closed briefly, as if there was too much sensation in him to take in any more. A shudder ran through Julie, and she stepped forward, her arms going around his neck, and stretched up to kiss him.

Their kiss was like a spark to tinder, and suddenly the passion, never far beneath the surface, flamed up. They kissed hungrily, fiercely, and in that instant everything else melted away. There were no reservations, no fears. Only the heat of their bodies and the shattering sensations running though them. Julie clung to Tag as if she could meld herself with him.

He crushed her to him, pressing her into his body. He wanted to feel her bare skin against him, her breasts pushing against his chest, nothing between them. But he could not release her long enough to remove her clothes. His hand slid down to grasp her hips and move her suggestively against him. The movement sent desire exploding through him, and he shuddered under the force of it. He had wanted her for weeks now, from the first moment he saw her, and now all those pent-up longings were released and coursing madly though him. In that moment Tag knew there was no end to his desire, that he could not take her quickly enough, thoroughly enough, hard enough. The hunger in him was wild and raging, his need acute.

He turned, lifting Julie in his arms, and carried her to the bed. He set her down on the mattress and quickly lay down with her, his mouth and hands seeking her again. They kissed deeply. Julie's hands roamed his bare back, sinking into the swell and dip of his muscles, tracing the bony outcroppings of his spine. Her fingers moved up to comb through his hair, delighting in the contrast of his hard skull and thick, soft hair. His scent was in her nostrils, his taste in her mouth. There was nothing but him and her fierce hunger.

Still, she wanted more. She wanted to feel his skin against hers, his hard body pressing into her. With a soft noise of frustration, she pulled her hands from his body and began to struggle with the buttons of her blouse. Tag slid half off her, giving her access to the fastenings, though he did not release her or stop their deep kisses. His tongue roamed her mouth. His hands clenched in the mass of her hair, savoring its silkiness.

"You're beautiful. Beautiful," he murmured, his lips making their heated, nibbling way across her cheekbone and down to the shell of her ear. He took the lobe into his mouth, gently sucking, then teased the sensitive flesh with his teeth.

Shivers coursed through Julie at the touch of his mouth on her ear. She fumbled at her blouse, practically ripping the last button from its moorings in her haste. She yanked the blouse out of her jeans, opening it to Tag, and immediately his hand was there, skimming over her skin. He cupped her breast, still covered with the thin material of her brassiere. His fingers slid over the soft cloth, feeling the curve and softness of her breast beneath it, the enticing hard bud of her nipple, but were denied the satiny texture of her skin. It aroused him, frustrated him, made him want to rip the clothes away and sink deep into her.

Tag clenched his teeth, struggling to regain the control that was rapidly spinning away from him. He had to go more slowly. Julie was inexperienced, and he had sworn to make it good for her. Gentle. God, he felt anything but gentle at the moment! He felt as wild as any male animal about to claim his mate.

With an effort he pulled himself away from her. Resting on his elbow, he gazed down at her, waiting for some remnant of calm and reason to return to him. But it was no easier to look at her than it had been to touch her. She made such a sweet and sexy picture lying there beneath him, her blouse spread out around her, her breasts cupped by the sensuously feminine bra. Her nipples popped up like hard little buttons, stretching the material, barely shadowed by the lace. He remembered how he had taken her nipple in his mouth before, material and all. The lace had scratched erotically against his tongue. Just recalling it sent another wave of heat pulsing through him.

He curved his hand around one breast and circled the nipple with his forefinger, watching the path of his finger and the effect of his touch upon her. Her skin grew more flushed; the nipple stretched up eagerly. He laid his hand on her chest and slid it beneath the top of the brassiere, stealing down to cup her breast. Then he pushed the cloth down, exposing her breast to his gaze and touch. The brassiere, taut beneath her breast, pushed it upward, almost as if offering it for his pleasure. Tag bent and lightly kissed her nipple, then straightened, watching how the fleshy nub puckered.

Again his mouth came down and this time he ran the tip of his tongue around the nipple again and again, discovering its taste and texture. Julie dug her fingers into the bed, clutching the spread. Tag smiled to himself at her response. Softly he blew on the wet nipple, and it tightened still further. Julie gasped at the new sensation.

"Oh, Tag... please," she whispered.

"I try to please," he said huskily. "Didn't I? Then perhaps this will." He lashed her nipple gently with his tongue.

Julie gave a low groan, and her legs moved restlessly on the bed. Tag laid his hand on her bare stomach and moved his fingers down, popping the snap of her jeans and sliding beneath them. She started at the intimate touch, her hips coming up off the bed. Tag pulled her nipple into his mouth, sucking it. His tongue roamed the soft breast around it. His hand slipped further down, seeking the heat of her femininity.

Julie panted his name, her hands moving over his shoulders and arms, coming up to tangle in his hair. "Now," she murmured, her hips moving unconsciously. "Please, Tag, I want you."

He groaned against her breast. "I want you, too. But not yet. Today you have to be very ready."

"I am."

"No. I've just begun. There's more, much more."

Tag sat up and reached behind her, unhooking her bra and pulling it off. Julie hastened to undress completely, kicking off her shoes and unzipping her jeans. Tag shucked off his own jeans, then helped Julie shove hers down off her legs. She started to remove her panties, as well, but he laid a hand on her, stopping her.

"No, wait. I'll do it."

Julie didn't protest. She was too busy looking at Tag's naked form. A few minutes earlier she would have been embarrassed, but now any embarrassment was overshadowed by the deep, throbbing ache within her. The sight of his long legs and lean torso, his hard and swollen masculinity, only increased that ache. Trembling slightly, her fingers drifted up his arm and down his chest. She wanted to go lower, but she didn't dare. Not yet. Instead she explored his chest, combing through the black curls and teasing the flat masculine nipples to life.

Tag closed his eyes, aroused almost past bearing by her light touch. His fingers curled inward, nails digging into his palms, using the pain to rein in the raging desire. There was time, plenty of time. Some other day he would take her fast and hard, glorying in the burst of passion.

But not today. Today was Julie's first time, and it had to be sweet and long.

He trailed his hand over her body, curving around the plump globes of her breasts and down over her stomach, coming at last to the flimsy barrier of her panties. He moved down over the slick material, caressing her through it. His fingers slipped beneath the waistband, teasing the tender skin across her stomach. In the same manner he eased his finger beneath the elastic of each leg, approaching but not actually touching the hot center of her passion. With each caress Julie grew hotter and more aching. In desperation she reached down and took his hand, pressing it against the juncture of her legs.

A tremor shook him, and he groaned. He began to kiss her neck, nibbling and caressing, while his hand stroked slowly up and down, rubbing the soft material of her panties against her. His mouth moved lower until it reached her breast, and he began to suckle it, his fingers all the while working their magic.

Julie was flooded with desire, awash in the delightful sensations Tag evoked in her. She reveled in the feelings. Yet with each new caress, she yearned even more for satisfaction, for the completion of their union, as if with every passing moment she was wound tighter and tighter, until she thought she would explode.

Tag hooked his hand in her panties and drew them down her legs. He tossed them aside, and his hand returned to her bare skin, retracing the movements he had made earlier over the material. His fingers teased downward to the hot damp crevice, tantalizing her by circling around the molten center, coming closer and closer, but never quite reaching it. Julie let out a little whimper and braced her feet against the bed, unconsciously pushing her hips up, urging him to go further.

At last he did. His mouth trailed down her body to kiss the soft plane of her stomach, and as he did so, his fingers slid into the slick folds of her femininity. Julie gasped, tightening all over, shaken by the primitive excitement that darted through her. She had never known anything like this intimate touch. Passion surged through her, heating her skin.

Gently Tag explored her. His finger slipped inside her in a foreshadowing of the full possession he would soon take. Julie's head rolled from side to side. She was lost in her need, incapable of holding anything back.

"Now," she whispered. "Please. I want you."

"Not enough," he replied hoarsely, his own control barely hanging by a thread. He continued to stroke her, to caress the tiny nub that sent desire like a shock all through her. Gradually he opened her up to him.

Finally he moved over her, and Julie opened her legs to him eagerly. Slowly, carefully, he began to enter her. Julie's eyes widened in surprise at just how much he widened and stretched her. Yet it was a gloriously fulfilling sensation, as well. She wanted to feel him filling her, wanted to take him in, to know him to the deepest core of her being. It seemed as if she had waited all her life for this moment, this feeling.

A flash of pain stabbed her, and then he was deep inside her. Tag had felt her tighten at the pain, and he stopped, sternly keeping his desire in check. She relaxed, and he moved again. Slowly, gently. Julie's arms went around him, and she began to move in rhythm with his thrusts. With each long, slow stroke, her passion grew, the excitement building in her to an ever more feverish pitch, until at last it exploded within her. She trembled under the force of it, and Tag's thrusts grew wild and frantic, sweeping both of them into a brief moment of unity, dark and sweet and formless.

Tag relaxed all over, and for a moment they lay together, drained and exhausted. Floating in a haze of pleasure. He shifted his weight from her and rolled over, slipping an arm around her to pull her close. Julie nestled into the hollow of his shoulder. She felt utterly spent and deliciously content. No, it was more than contentment. There was joy in her, too, and a remembered excitement.

She thought about what she had told Tag earlier, that she was afraid she might fall in love with him. Now she knew that it was too late. She was already in love with him. And right now that idea didn't scare her one bit. It felt wonderful.

Chapter 9

Tag smoothed back a strand of hair that had fallen across Julie's cheek and clung there. "Are you all right?" he asked softly and kissed the top of her head. "Did I hurt you?"

Julie smiled to herself. "Not enough to notice."

His hand curved over her cheek and moved down her neck and shoulders. "Good. I'm glad. I got a little carried away there at the end, and I was afraid..."

"Don't worry," she reassured him. "I enjoyed it when you got carried away." She propped herself up on her elbow and looked into his face. "Why didn't you tell me it would be like this? I didn't know. I wasn't prepared." She grinned impishly. "We could have started doing this earlier."

Julie's eyes were shining, her face delicately tinted with color, her lips moist and well-kissed. She looked so lovely and so sensual that, incredibly, Tag felt desire begin to stir in him again.

He reached up to trace his forefinger across her lips. "You wouldn't have believed me."

"That's probably true. It's something that has to be experienced." She lay back down, dropping a light kiss on his shoulder and snuggling into him. There was a moment of languid silence, then Julie said, "Tag?"

"Mmm?"

"Is it always like this? Or was it just us?"

"It was special." He caressed her arm lightly. "But I have the feeling that between us it'll always be special.

"I'm being dumb, aren't I?" Julie was sure that a more sophisticated woman wouldn't ask such questions. She would simply know. But even that knowledge couldn't spoil her mood.

"No. You're not being dumb. You're simply an open, honest woman. There's nothing wrong with that."

They dozed for a while, and when they awakened, they were famished. "Shall we go out?" Tag asked Julie, and she shook her head.

"No. Let's eat in." There was still a languid, sated look on her face. "I'd rather not be around people tonight."

"I agree. I don't want to be with anyone but you." Tag got out of bed a little reluctantly. He stretched, bending a little to one side and then the other. "Lord, my muscles are already getting stiff from that work today. I swear, since I moved here I've discovered muscles I never knew I had before."

"Take a nice hot bath," Julie advised. "Then I'll rub your back, if you want."

He slanted an impish look at her. "That'll make the pain worthwhile."

Tag pulled on his trousers and found a short terry-cloth robe for Julie to wear. She slipped out of bed, a trifle self-conscious at being naked in front of him, then wrapped the robe around herself and belted it. It was far too big, but it smelled like Tag, and she felt wrapped in his warmth.

They went to the kitchen and slapped together a meal, laughing and joking as they did. Now and then they stopped what they were doing to kiss, and once the kiss stretched into a long series of kisses and caresses, until finally Julie pulled back, flushed and smiling, reminding Tag that they would never finish if they didn't stop.

Both of them were ravenous, and they ate heartily. Julie discovered that she even enjoyed watching Tag eat. When they finished, he suggested a soak in the hot tub on the patio, but when Julie started out to the pool house for a swimsuit, he reached out a hand to stop her.

"There's no need," he told her. "You're fine like you are."

"But I don't—" Julie stopped. "You mean get in without any clothes on?"

"Sure. Why not? There's no one around to see you. Except me." His smile left no doubt as to how intently he would be watching her.

Excitement rose in her even as she flushed a little in embarrassment. "All right."

He turned the hot tub on, and when it was warm they shed their clothes and got in. Julie felt decidedly odd, being stark naked outdoors. But is also made her a little breathless. Had she gone crazy? Was this actually her? Sensible, responsible Julie Farrell—climbing into a hot tub without a stitch of clothing on—and in the company of an equally naked man?

It was crazy. Yet she had never felt this happy or alive before.

The warm water was soothing, and she leaned back against the lounge-type seat. Across from her, Tag sat on a similar seat, facing her. She began to relax. They talked lazily about any and everything, and her shyness drifted away. The water bubbled around her. She marveled at how much nicer it felt on her bare skin than through a swimsuit. The bubbles teased across her slightly tender nipples and caressed her stomach and hips.

A silence fell over them, and Julie glanced across at Tag. He was watching her, lids drooping over his bright eyes, and the expression on his face sizzled right through her. Her breath caught in her throat. He stood up and crossed the narrow space between them, reaching down to pull Julie to her feet.

As she stood, the water lapped under her breasts. Her nipples tightened as the air touched them. Tag looked down at her breasts. A drop caught on one of the nipples and clung there, and he bent and scooped the droplet up with his tongue.

He lifted her up, his arms crossed beneath her buttocks, until her breasts were on a level with his mouth. He laved the pink-brown nipples with his tongue, and the sensitized buds hardened. Tag lifted his head and stared into her eyes. "I would like," he said softly, "to take you about a hundred different ways."

"I didn't know there were that many," she answered breathlessly.

"I'd think of them." He kissed each of her breasts in turn, then set her down, and they climbed hand-in-hand out of the tub.

Julie expected him to turn toward the house and the bedroom, but instead he led her to the pool. The pale water was deliciously cool against their heated skin. It flowed over her body like a caress. She turned on her back, floating, and Tag slid his arms beneath her, holding her in place. He bent his head and feasted on her breasts. Julie released a sigh of pure pleasure. His hand came up between her legs and explored the water-slick flesh.

He caressed her gently, lightly, arousing her with every movement of his hand, every tug of his mouth on her breasts. Julie felt as if she were floating in sensation, weightless, mindless, feeling nothing but pure physical pleasure. Her legs moved apart, silently asking for the complete fulfillment only Tag could give. But still his hands and mouth played upon her, and her pleasure built until it was almost unbearable. And then it rolled through her, shattering her, and she stiffened, shuddering, kept up only by Tag's hands beneath her.

Finally he moved between her legs and slid into her tender flesh. She moaned at the feel of him against her sensitized skin. It was a pleasure so great it was akin to pain. His hands were beneath her back, holding her afloat; as he began to move, his fingers dug into her. He struggled to retain his control amidst the turbulent passion swirling within him. He moved in and out slowly, rebuilding Julie's desire to its peak even as he pushed himself almost past sanity.

A shudder took him, and he groaned as their desire exploded within them both, hurtling them into a hot, dark realm of wild sensation.

When he left her, they floated in the water for a while, side by side, fingers touching, too enervated to move. Later Tag picked Julie up and carried her from the pool, going only a short distance to one of the loungers. He lay down, snuggling her tightly to him, and wrapped a beach towel around them both. The cool evening air caressed their skin. The stars and moon glistened in the deep black sky above them. And Julie lay against his chest, hearing the heavy thud of his heart, enveloped in a cocoon of love.

For the next few weeks, hardly a day went by that Julie didn't see Tag. He dropped by the store often to see her, surprising her with a lunch or talking her into taking a break with him. They walked along the creek that ran through the park at the edge of the town. They meandered through the video store, aimlessly shopping as a cover for the real purpose of their visit, holding hands and being together, looking at each other with a smile or a whisper. Tag even went with her to the grocery store once or twice, pushing the cart and making absurd suggestions about what items to take from the shelves.

He spent many evenings at her house, sometimes joining in cooking a meal, other times playing cards with her and her family, or simply watching TV and talking. Julie was surprised to see that Tag didn't seem bothered or put out about having her brother and sister around. He joked and talked with them as if he'd known them all his life. It wasn't long before Cathy adored him, and even the reticent Riley opened up and talked to him.

"I like him," Riley said to Julie one day. "I can talk to him about books and my ideas, and he doesn't think I'm weird."

Once they went to a dance at the SPJST Hall in Horton. Run by the local Czech society, the hall was open to anyone, and people from miles around came there to dance. A band played country and western music, and couples two-stepped around a large dance floor sprinkled with sand. Folding tables and chairs were set around the walls of the large room, occupied by couples and even families. A concession booth at the back of the hall sold beer, soft drinks, hot dogs and chips.

Tag looked around the dance hall in amazement, taking in the dancers in jeans, boots and cowboy hats, and the children dancing together or alone on the edge of the dance floor, or playing tag around the corners of the room. "What a place!" he murmured. He glanced at Julie. "I've never seen anything quite like it."

She wasn't surprised when her grandfather walked in about an hour later. This dance hall was one of his and Riette's favorite places. Horace spotted them and waved exuberantly, then led Riette over to the table where Tag and Julie sat.

"Well, say, how're you kids doing?" he asked cheerfully.

"Great," Tag answered, grinning. He always enjoyed Horace. "Sit down and join us."

"Why, sure. Riette, honey, this is Tag Marshall, Julie's boyfriend." Julie cringed at the expression he used to describe Tag. "Tag, this is Riette Walker, the prettiest lady in the county."

Riette giggled and playfully swatted Horace's arm. "Oh, Horace, you say the silliest things."

Riette was in her fifties, a good fifteen or twenty years younger than Horace, though she, too, was a grandparent. She was a widow and leased out the farmland her husband had left her while she worked part-time in the local drugstore. Her hair was dyed red, the color it had been before it started turning gray, and she covered the ravages time had brought to her face with the liberal application of makeup. She was fighting a losing battle with middle-age weight gain, but her buxom figure still looked good in the scoop-necked peasant blouse and full denim skirt she wore. There was nothing Riette loved like going honky-tonking and dancing, and she and Horace had been a steady item for the past two or three years. Neither of them ever thought about marrying. They had their lives arranged exactly the way they wanted them.

They spent the evening at Tag and Julie's table, and the younger couple found that they could barely keep up with them on the dance floor. Off the dance floor Horace was full of his usual quips and jokes, and kept them all laughing.

"Who would ever have thought you could go out with your girlfriend's *grandparents* and have a good time?" Tag marveled to Julie as they sat watching Horace and Riette twirl around the room in a lively polka.

But Julie found Tag the astonishing one. What other man, especially a wealthy, sophisticated city dweller, would have an uproarious time in a little rural dance hall with a pair of senior citizens?

Tag even accompanied Julie to programs at school and to most of Cathy's FFA shows. Late in October they drove up to watch Cathy show her steer in the state fair. Looking over at Tag as they sat in the bleachers, watching Cathy guide Clown around the arena, Julie was amazed at how easily he fit in, how little there was in him of an Eastern snob. Later they roamed the fair, taking in the midway rides and games, and exhibit buildings, eating corn dogs and popcorn and cotton candy.

But that evening Tag took Julie back to the luxurious downtown hotel in which they were staying, since Cathy was rooming with her FFA group overnight. They bathed and changed into evening clothes, and he took her out to dinner at an elegant restaurant, then on to the touring Broadway musical playing at the fair, and finally to the top of the revolving tower of the Hyatt for late-night drinks. When they finally returned to the hotel room, they made long, languorous love on the wide bed and fell asleep in each other's arms.

It was a strange sensation to wake up in bed beside Tag. They had never slept together the whole night through, for Julie had always insisted that she go home after they had made love, so she could be there if the kids needed her. But unusual as it was, it was anything but unpleasant. Tag ordered room service, and they ate breakfast in bed, which seemed like an almost decadent luxury to Julie. Afterwards they made love again before getting up to leisurely bathe and dress for the journey back to Brinkman.

"I liked that," Tag mused later as they sped down I-35 toward Austin. His hand lay over Julie's on the seat between them.

"What?" She turned her head and smiled at him. Just looking at Tag made her heart expand with joy. She was realizing more and more each day just how madly in love with him she was. She told herself it was foolish and dangerous to lose her heart so completely to this man, but reason had no sway with her any longer, it seemed. There was too much happiness in her to leave room for worry or doubt.

"Waking up with you in the morning. Waking up in the middle of the night and feeling you cuddled up against my back." He picked up her hand and brought it to his lips for a tender kiss. "I wish it were that way all the time."

Her hand tightened reflexively. "Tag, you know how I feel about staying at your house all night with Riley and Cathy at home. I can't do it."

"I didn't mean staying out with me all night. I meant staying home all night. I—"

Julie's eyes widened. "You mean you staying at our house? Oh, no, I—"

"Would you let me finish before you jump to conclusions? I meant *us* staying at *our* house. Julie...oh, this is a hell of a way to be saying this." He took an exit ramp off the highway and pulled to a stop on the side of the access road. He cut off the engine and turned toward her, his face serious. "Julie, I want to marry you."

She stared at him. "What?"

"I want us to get married."

"But we hardly know each other. I mean, it's only been a couple of months since I met you. It's too fast."

"Do I have to wait five months before I can tell you I want to get married? A person knows when it's right, and I know. I love you. I want to marry you. It doesn't matter whether I've known you two months or two weeks or all my life. I don't want to live away from you. I don't want to visit you, to be your lover only when you can get away for a few hours. This morning I realized how nice, how special, it was to have you with me, morning and night. To see your face first thing when I wake up. To share breakfast with you. I even liked having your makeup and brush lying there on the counter beside my stuff.''

Julie continued to gaze at him, astonished. This was so far from anything she had ever expected Tag to say that she had trouble assimilating it. For the past few weeks she had been falling more and more in love with him each day, always dreading what would happen when it was time for him to go home. She had tried to prepare herself for his telling her that he was leaving, that she would never see him again. But she hadn't wasted a moment's thought on preparing herself for a marriage proposal!

Tag frowned, and there was a flicker of uncertainty in his eyes. ''Julie? I'm sorry. Have I assumed too much? I thought you felt the same way I do.''

''I did! I do! I mean…oh, Tag, yes, I love you. I've loved you for weeks and weeks, practically from the moment I first saw you. But I—I didn't expect you to ask me anything like this! I'm stunned.''

''How could you not have any idea how I felt? I *told* you! Did you think I usually spend every spare moment with someone in whom I have only a slight interest?''

''I don't know what I thought about it all. I assumed that eventually you would go back to North Carolina and I would lose you.'' Tears welled up in

Julie's eyes, and she dashed them away in irritation. "I'm sorry. I managed not to cry at thinking you were going to leave me, and here I am, tearing up when you tell me you aren't!"

"I'll take it as a positive sign," he said gently as he reached out and curved his hand over her cheek.

Julie gave a funny little gasp, almost a sob, and suddenly she was across the seat and in his arms, her face buried against his neck. He felt the dampness of her tears against his skin, and he wrapped his arms tightly around her and kissed her hair.

"Shh. Sweetheart, what's the matter?"

"I don't know! I think—I think I'm happy!"

He smiled lovingly and rubbed his cheek against her head. "I think I'm happy, too. At least, I think I would be if you'd answer my question. Will you marry me?"

Julie kissed his neck. He felt the faint tremor in her lips, and it sent a fierce, strange surge of sensation through him—part desire, part protectiveness. Julie was usually so much in control, so in charge of herself and any situation, that this sudden vulnerability was somehow alluring.

"I love you," she whispered. "I want to marry you."

"Do I hear a 'but' in there?" He shifted, lifting her away from him so he could look into her eyes. "Are you about to turn me down gently?"

She shook her head, one hand going to her face to shove back her hair. "I don't know what I'm about to do. I want to marry you. More than anything." It was true. The urge to say yes to him pulsed inside her, barely held in check by the restraints of reason. "But I'm not sure it's the right thing."

"What's not right about it? You love me. I love you. I want to live with you for the rest of my life. Is that what you want, too?"

"Yes." Her clear-eyed gaze validated her words. "But, Tag, I have other things I have to consider. Other people I have to think about. I can't jump into something just because I want to."

"What's the problem?"

"What about Cathy and Riley? There's the rest of this year. Riley will go off to college after that, but he still needs a home and someone to—to look after him. Cathy will be in high school for two more years. They're my responsibility. I can't just run off and leave them."

"I never thought you would. You want them to come live with us? Okay." He raised one mobile eyebrow in that way he had. "Or do you want me to join the menagerie at your house?" He tilted his head, considering. "I guess I could handle that."

"God, no. One more person using that bathroom upstairs is all we need. But I figured you wouldn't want the kids with us."

He shrugged. "Hell, yes. Lyle, too, if he wants. There's plenty of room." He continued, his tone more serious. "I like them all. Sure, I'd prefer to have you to myself. But I understand. I wouldn't ask you to desert your family. I know you better than to think you would do something like that. Besides, I enjoy them. Even Horace. I feel as if I'm part of a family when I'm at your house. I think I like it better than the family I grew up with."

"You're serious? You'd take Riley and Cathy in, too?" He nodded. Relief flooded Julie, and she kissed him hard on the mouth. "I love you. You're the best man in the world."

"I imagine there are some who'd dispute that."

"I don't care about them."

"Then will you marry me?"

"Oh, yes." Julie threw her arms around him. "Yes, I'll marry you."

In the first rush of happiness Julie didn't think about anything but the joy of her love, the excitement of marrying Tag. It was only later that she began to consider the ramifications of marrying him. It was wonderful and for him to say that Cathy and Riley could live with them seemed to solve her problems. But *where* were they going to live?

Surely Tag would want to move back to North Carolina. After all, that was where his family was, his home, his friends, all his interests. Could she bear to move? Even the thought of it made her feel sad. This was her home. It was where she wanted to stay. And she knew that Cathy would want to stay, and even Riley, who professed to hate Brinkman, wouldn't want to leave until he finished high school. They would want to finish school here. Cathy would have to have her animals. They would rather stay at home with Granddad than move with her to a city in North Carolina. Wouldn't she be dropping her responsibility to them just as much as she would have been if Tag hadn't wanted her family to live with them?

Yet it would be selfish and unfair of her to insist that Tag live here, where she was comfortable and at home. How could she insist that he abandon his home? He had already invited her siblings and Granddad to live with them. That was as much generosity as anyone could expect. She couldn't demand to have everything her own way. Marriage was a compromise.

She didn't want to lose Tag. But she didn't want to have to choose her home over him, either. Much as she loved Brinkman, she loved Tag more. Surely she would get used to living in North Carolina. She had heard it was beautiful. Maybe they could live a little way out in the country instead of right next to other people, and she could raise a few animals. Tag loved to ride. He would probably be happy to live where he could keep his horse instead of having to stable him.

Julie didn't mention her reservations to anyone. Everyone in her family was so excited about their marriage that she didn't want to spoil their happiness by mentioning doubts. She was scared to bring the matter up with Tag; afraid that once she did, she would actually have to make the awful choice. She didn't want to. She didn't want to have to face it. It was easier to let it slide, to hope that somehow the problem would resolve itself without her having to make a decision.

Once or twice Tag started to talk about where they would live after they were married, but Julie was always quick to cut him off. It was far easier to make sure they veered off onto another subject or to divert Tag with a kiss or a caress that soon ended with them in bed together and oblivious to everything but the joy of their lovemaking.

About a week after they became engaged, Tag suggested that they fly to North Carolina to visit his family. Julie turned wide, almost frightened eyes on him. "What?"

"I said, why don't we go to Winston-Salem next week? I want my family to meet you. I'm sure Mother will insist on throwing some kind of party to celebrate." He grinned. "No doubt my father will be ecstatic to hear that I'm actually going to get married."

Julie wasn't so sure about that. Mr. Marshall might be ecstatic for Tag to marry some local society girl, but that didn't mean he was going to welcome with open arms an ordinary, middle-class woman from Brinkman, Texas. She thought that he was more likely to accuse Tag of trying to ruin the family. From what Tag had said about the man, she had built up an imposing picture of Leith Marshall in her mind, and she couldn't imagine that patriarchal figure being happy to have a country girl who sold feed for a living as his future daughter-in-law.

"So soon?" she asked, casting about in her mind for a reason not to go.

"Why not?" He looked at her more closely. "What's the matter? Don't you want to meet them?"

"Of course I do. I mean, in a way. I'd like to see them, find out what they're like and everything..."

"But?"

"But I'm scared."

"Scared!" He looked astonished. "Is this the same woman I saw chop off the head of a snake with a shovel last week?"

Julie made a face. "That's not the same thing. What if they don't like me? What if they think I'm not good enough for a Marshall?"

"They won't." He went to her and took her hands in his. "Trust me. They'll all wonder how I managed to land anybody as lovely and down-to-earth and nice as you."

"Oh, Tag . . ."

"You wait. You'll see. They'll be whispering to each other, 'How did Tag find someone so normal? And what does she see in him?'" He mimicked a high-pitched voice of astonishment, and Julie had to giggle.

"You're a terrible liar."

"I am not! It's the truth. Anyway, suppose they don't like you? So what? It won't make a bit of difference to me and the way I feel about you. You aren't marrying my family. You're marrying me. In case you've forgotten."

Julie smiled, warmed by his words despite her remaining uneasiness over meeting his family. "Oh, yeah, that's right." She stretched up to give him a brief kiss on the lips. "Okay. Let's go visit your family. Might as well get it over with."

Tag grinned. "That's often been my sentiment exactly."

"Tell me about your family." Julie settled back comfortably on the couch, pulling her knees up to sit cross-legged. They were at her house, waiting in the den while the fudge she had made earlier for a school bake sale cooled in its pan in the kitchen. "You've never said much about them except how you and your father don't get along."

"Well, let's see. There's my father, who is an excellent attorney and a man of importance, and that pretty much sums up his personality. Then there's my mother, Joyce. She's very attractive for her age. She always has been. She's big into charity functions and teas and lunch at the Club. She also likes antiques. Their house is full of them—very tastefully arranged, of course."

"Of course."

"I've told you about Gran Taggart."

"The one you used to spend summers with?"

"Yeah." He smiled faintly. "She's great. Still as warm and friendly and down-to-earth as she was before she married into Taggart Mills. On the other side is Grandmother Marshall, who's one of those slim, white-haired martriarchs. My father's scared to death of her, I think. Both my grandfathers are dead."

"What about your brothers?"

"Adam is the oldest. He's an attorney, as well. He's into civil litigation. He's quite good, but he's not consumed by it like Father. Adam's the best of the lot, and he's married to a wonderful woman. Emily. She was his secretary, and was once a real wallflower. I used to go by and talk to her whenever I went to see Adam. Then, all of a sudden, she blossomed. Practically overnight. Adam never would tell me the whole story, but I got the feeling her transformation had something to do with him."

"It sounds romantic."

He smiled. "I'm sure it was. Emily's the kind of woman who has romantic written all over her. You'll like her. *She* was no debutante, and the family loves her. Adam had a bad first marriage and divorce. We were all grateful to see him wind up with someone as nice as Emily the second time around. Last, but not least, there's James."

"What's the matter with James?"

"Nothing. Why?"

"There was an odd note in your voice when you said his name. Don't you all get along?"

"James and I are very different. When we were kids we were always getting into fights, and Adam would have to separate us. We don't fight anymore. We get along okay. We're just not . . . real close, I guess. He's a serious person, and he thinks I'm frivolous. I think he's rigid. I mean, he's a good man. You'd have to look hard to find anyone more honest or dedicated or hard-working. He's a federal prosecutor, and he really believes in what he does. He despises fraud and dishonesty, prejudice. He's a strict upholder of the law.''

"He sounds like a prig."

Tag laughed. "No, he's not, really. He has a sense of humor. He's good-looking, with a nice personality. A lot of women fall for him. But he's tough, he sees things as being strictly black and white, without much room for grays. He's a fighter. He'd go to the wall for any of us. But he's not the easiest person in the world to be with. His job comes first. I think that's why he's never married. I love him, but I've always felt that he thought I was something of a disappointment."

Julie's chin came up pugnaciously. "Well, maybe *he's* the disappointment."

Tag chuckled, but her loyalty warmed him. "How refreshing. Now *I* have a defender."

"Of course. And you always will have.

"I like that," Tag murmured and leaned over to kiss her lips. "I like that a lot. You know, if we weren't already engaged, I'd ask you to marry me."

"You know what? I'd accept."

He kissed her again, and all thought of his family, their trip, or anything else fled her mind.

Chapter 10

Tag and Julie flew from Austin to North Carolina the following Friday. She remembered Tag's anxiety about flying and held tightly to his hand every time the plane lifted off or landed. Tag, realizing what she was doing, shot her a rueful smile and raised her hand to his lips to kiss it.

"Trying to keep me from getting drunk?" he asked.

She shook her head, reminded of her misconception about his drinking when she first met him. "No. I just thought maybe it would help."

"It does. Having you with me always helps, no matter what's going on."

They landed several hours later. Julie glanced around, expecting to see some member of Tag's family there to meet them, but he steered straight through the crowd of greeters, hardly glancing at any of them. He led her down the hall and through the lobby to the baggage claim area. She thought it odd that no one had come to pick them up. She couldn't imagine returning from a trip and not finding at least one of her siblings or Granddad there. Perhaps this was more common when one was used to flying as Tag was. Still...

Tag steered her through the baggage claim area and out onto the sidewalk. An elegant old tobacco-brown Rolls Royce sat by the curb. As they stepped outside, a tall, thin black man emerged from the driver's seat, smiling. "Mr. Marshall." He walked toward them. "It's nice to see you again."

"Hey, Dokes. What's this Mr. Marshall stuff?" He turned to Julie. "This from the man who used to tan my hide regularly for playing on Grandmother Marshall's car."

"It was well-deserved, too," Dokes added affectionately. "I was trying to be polite, Taggart. I thought you might want to impress your young lady."

"Nah. She knows me too well. Julie, I'd like you to meet Dokes Baker. He has the distinct honor of having worked for my grandmother for over twenty years, the one person I know of who has managed to get along with her that long."

The older man grinned. "Now, don't you go bad-mouthing your grandmama. She's a nice lady. It just takes a little diplomacy to get along with her, that's all."

"Then you ought to work for the State Department. She's never kept any other employee longer than a year or two. Dokes, allow me to introduce you to Julie Farrell of Brinkman, Texas. She's a very special young lady."

"I can see that for myself." He smiled at Julie. "I'm pleased to meet you, Miss Farrell."

"Oh, please, Julie." She held out her hand. "I won't know who you're talking to if you call me Miss Farrell. I'm pleased to meet you, too."

"How did you get roped in to coming to pick us up?" Tag asked as they walked toward the car.

"Your mother needed someone to run errands for her today, what with you coming in and the dinner tonight and the party at the country club tomorrow, so Mrs. Marshall sent me over to help out." Dokes opened the back door for them. "You two get in the car, and I'll get your bags."

"That's okay, I'll do it," Tag offered as he helped Julie into the spacious back seat. "You won't recognize Julie's luggage. You sit here with Julie and keep her entertained. Tell her embarrassing stories about my family or something."

Dokes closed the door, and Julie settled back gingerly into the luxurious leather seat. The car was beautiful on the inside, all supple tan leather and burled walnut paneling. Glass separated the driver from the passengers, and a small bar was mounted on one wall. Julie was almost afraid to touch anything for fear she would hurt the elegant interior.

Dokes didn't tell her stories about the family or anyone else. Instead he rolled down the divider and fussed over whether she was warm and comfortable enough. Julie couldn't imagine *not* being comfortable in such a roomy, plush car. Why, the seat was softer than any chair in her house.

Tag returned with the luggage, and they started toward Winston-Salem. The airport was actually in Greensboro, some thirty miles away from the city, so it was a long drive to Tag's home. As they reached the city Tag began to point out and name the various

points of interest. "There's Taggart Mills—the low
building on the edge with the twin smokestacks. And
the Reynolds building, that's the little one that looks
like the Empire State building. Wachovia. North
Carolina National Bank. And that blue glass thing is
Allied Central, my uncle's bank."

Julie listened quietly, feeling a little overwhelmed.
It seemed so strange to be sitting there talking about
the family bank, the family textile mill. What had it
been like to grow up knowing that this or that city
landmark was owned by your family? She couldn't
quite imagine being a Marshall of the Winston-Salem
Marshalls.

Tag was continuing. "Marshall, Pierson, etcetera,
is in the Allied Building, too."

"Your father and brother's law firm?"

"Yeah, Dad and Adam. You'll get to meet them all.
I'm sure Mother'll have some kind of big to-do in
honor of your visit."

"Oh, no, that's not necessary," Julie protested,
filled with horror at the vision of meeting a roomful
of well-heeled, well-read and well-spoken Marshalls
and Taggarts, all of them looking down their noses at
the country mouse of a girl who'd dared to become
involved with one of their own.

"Sure it is," Tag responded cheerfully. "I'm sure
Mother's dying to do it. They're all eaten up with curiosity about this 'Texas girl' I've brought home, if I
know anything about my family."

Julie was sure they were. It didn't make her feel any
more comfortable.

They left the expressway and turned onto a broad,
tree-lined street. Huge houses sat well back from the
road. Dokes turned in at a white, columned, South-

ern-style mansion. They drove up a long driveway to the house. Julie sat speechless, staring. Her stomach had dropped to her feet. You couldn't get much farther from her own plain farmhouse than this. Had Tag actually grown up in this house?

For the first time the real significance of his wealthy life-style began to sink in on her. Tag was so easygoing and fit in so readily almost anywhere that most of the time she no longer thought of him as being a member of the upper crust. He acted just like anybody else. But obviously he wasn't and never had been.

Julie was suddenly scared. She wished she were back at home, safe in the store in Brinkman or out hauling hay to the pasture. The last thing she wanted to do was enter that mansion.

But she had no choice. The car had already come to a gentle stop, and Tag was getting out, pulling her after him. His face was eager, almost excited, and she knew that he was overjoyed to be home, back where he belonged.

An older woman, short and dumpy in a plain pink dress, opened the door at his ring. "Taggart, you handsome devil!" she cried and threw her arms around him.

Julie stared. Surely this couldn't be Taggart's mother, whom he had described as being the Queen of the Country Club. "Mary Louise!" Tag hugged her back hard. "You know I couldn't stay away from you." He released her and turned to Julie. "Julie, this is our housekeeper, Mary Louise Cooper."

"Well, I see you're as smooth-talking as ever, Taggart Marshall," the woman returned dryly before turning and welcoming Julie.

The housekeeper. Naturally. That was almost as good as the old family nurse. Who would pop up next, a graying English butler?

Instead it was his mother, a tall, slender woman dressed in a classically simple cream-colored wool shirtwaist. Her blond hair, sprinkled with a frosting of white, was swept back from her face and curled under in a smooth pageboy, from which Julie was sure not a hair would dare to escape. Her face was calm and beautifully made-up, laugh lines smoothed away with expensive lotions and creams.

"Taggart. Darling." She crossed the marble entry unhurriedly and reached up to place a peck on his cheek. "How nice to see you home again." She turned expectantly toward Julie. "And you must be Julie. I'm so happy to meet you. Taggart speaks very highly of you."

"Thank you." Julie's voice came out almost too soft to hear, and she had to clear her throat and try again. "It's nice to meet you, too."

"I'm sure you two will want to freshen up and rest before the dinner tonight. It's a small affair. Only family, of course. Still, one doesn't like to be too tired to enjoy it. Mary Louise will show you to your room, Julie. Taggart, you, of course, are in your old room. Now, if you will excuse me, I have a few things to see to. I'm glad that Taggart brought you the weekend of the club dance. Everyone will be delighted to get a chance to meet you."

"The club dance?" Julie asked sotto voce as they walked away toward the stairs.

"Yeah. They have them every so often. No big deal. We can slip away early if you want."

"No big deal!" Julie repeated in acid tones. "Tag, I didn't bring anything to wear to a fancy party! I bet it's long gowns and everything!"

"Well, yes," he admitted. "It *is* black tie."

"What am I going to wear?" Julie's stomach knotted as she thought of the meager contents of her suitcase. She had brought a couple of nice dresses, but they were the sort of things one wore to church or out to a nice restaurant, not at all what the crème de la crème of society would be wearing at a black-tie affair at the country club! Tag's mother would probably faint if Julie came down in her little gray jacketed dress.

Tag shrugged. "We'll run out and buy you something tomorrow. Plenty of time."

"Tag..." He was hopeless. He didn't understand that most people didn't run out and buy five hundred or thousand dollar dresses because they hadn't brought anything suitable for a dance.

They had reached the top of the stairs, lagging farther and farther behind Mary Louise as they talked. She stood waiting for them beside an open doorway on the right side of the stairs. As they approached she said, "This is your room, Julie."

Julie stepped past her into a spacious, beautiful room furnished with antique colonial pieces. It was perfectly done, from the four-poster bed right down to the brass candlesnuffer adorning the small secretary. "It's beautiful," she breathed, wondering how she was going to sleep in this elegantly coordinated room. She would be afraid to sit on the low chair with its damask-covered cushion, and to set any of her obviously modern belongings on the dresser would seem like sacrilege.

"I'm glad you like it." Mary Louise took the compliment as her right. "The bathroom is through that door." She pointed across the room. "Dinner is at eight, and I believe Mr. Marshall will be having cocktails at seven. If you need anything, please let me know."

"I will. Thank you."

The housekeeper left, and Tag followed Julie into the room. He pulled her into his arms. "I see that Mary Louise and Mama are trying to preserve your virtue."

"What do you mean?"

"My room is at the opposite end of the hall—beyond the master bedroom. I better have my way with you now," he teased, wiggling his eyebrows madly. "It may be my last chance."

He bent her theatrically back over his arm and kissed her. But there was no pretense in the kiss. It was deep and long. Julie could feel the heat blazing across his skin. He straightened, pulling her up against his chest, and kissed her again with the same passionate thoroughness.

By the time he released her, they were both breathless. "Oh, Tag." Julie drew in a shaky breath and stepped out of his arms. "We better stop. I mean, we can't do anything right here in your parents' house."

"I know." He reached out and softly stroked his hand down her cheek. "But, you know, it's damned hard, keeping my hands off you."

She cast him a sideways glance and grinned. "Well, you aren't the only one."

Desire sparked in his eyes, and he started toward her, hands outstretched. Julie slipped out of his reach and around the bedpost. "Oh, no, you don't. I'm not letting you get me into trouble with your parents."

He curved his hands around the bedpost between them and leaned closer. "All right, then. But you have to stop saying things like that to me."

"Like what?" She opened her eyes in a wide, innocent look.

"You know like what." His fingers moved slowly down the pole as he gazed steadily at her.

Julie felt the heat of his eyes all through her, and she couldn't look away from the hypnotic movement of his hands against the dark, polished wood. Her abdomen felt warm and liquid. She moved closer, putting one of her hands onto the bedpost beneath his. They looked at each other. Her hand slid up until it touched his.

He linked his fingers with hers and leaned forward against the post. Julie leaned forward, too. Their bodies were only inches apart, not touching except where their fingers twined together.

"Damn," he breathed. "I have a feeling this is going to be a long weekend." He pulled back reluctantly. "I better go."

Julie nodded. She didn't want him to leave. But she knew as well as he did that they couldn't possibly make love, not with his mother and the housekeeper downstairs. So she smiled weakly and watched him walk out of the room.

Julie dressed carefully for dinner. She had finally lain down on the bed and napped a little. When she awakened, she had taken a bath, and now she felt refreshed after a long flight. She had brought only a couple of dresses with her, so her wardrobe was limited, but Tag had warned her that his mother would probably arrange some sort of a dressy function, so she had brought along a suitable gray dress with a jacket. With a pair of delicate silver earrings and a silver chain, she thought it looked elegant enough for a Marshall dinner gathering.

Once she had dressed, made-up and perfumed, she paced the floor of her bedroom for several minutes, working up the courage to go downstairs and face Tag's family. Normally she was not a person who gave in to her fears, but right now she couldn't stop thinking about the fact that the Marshall men waiting below were all attorneys—and she hadn't even finished a year of college. The Marshalls had been to all kinds of places—and she'd hardly been outside the state of Texas. They'd grown up going to prep schools and attending extravagant parties—and she'd grown up going to Brinkman public schools and feeding cows. Every minute she'd been in North Carolina, from the moment they'd been met by the chauffeur in a Rolls to walking through this huge, exquisitely furnished house to just a little while ago when she'd peeked out the window and seen nothing but Mercedes and BMWs parked in the circular driveway—she had grown more and more certain that Tag's family would dislike her.

She had known that Tag had money. It was obvious in his clothes, his car, the sprawling ranch house. But somehow it was different at home. It was a familiar kind of wealth, land and cattle. And when Tag was sweating alongside the other workers, wearing boots and jeans and a plain cotton shirt, his money didn't seem to be an insurmountable barrier. But here, in this place, it struck her how very far away from her Tag really was. He came from a background, a life-style, that was utterly removed from her own. This was old money, Southern aristocracy, and his family couldn't be happy about his marrying an ordinary, unaristocratic woman like her.

A knock at the door jarred her from her dark thoughts. She went to open it and found Tag standing outside in the hall. Suddenly he looked almost like a stranger to her, too polished to be the man who made love to her with such passionate intensity.

"Hi." She forced a tremulous smile.

"Hi." He grinned down at her. "You look stunning. Ready to go?"

His smile was reassuring. "Yes. I guess so."

She stepped out of the room, and he took her hand, then glanced at her, startled. "Your hand's ice cold! What's the matter?"

"I'm scared," she confessed.

"Come on, they aren't that bad. Even Father isn't an ogre. I tell you, they'll like you. Even if they don't, they'll be terribly genteel and polite about it. They won't let you know."

"Oh, great. Now you're telling me that I won't be able to tell whether they like me or hate me."

Tag chuckled. "You're hopeless. Come on. Let's get it over with. Then you can relax."

"Pinch me if I do something wrong," she told him as they walked down the hall and started down the stairs. From below, the sound of a deep masculine laugh floated up to them.

"You won't do anything wrong. If you did, I probably wouldn't notice, anyway."

They rounded the curve of the staircase, and Julie saw several people standing below them in the large, open entryway. In her fear she was unable to separate them into individuals. They seemed a blur of impeccable hair and clothes and soft Southern accents.

"There you are, dear," Tag's mother said, looking up and seeing them. "Do come down and introduce Miss Farrell around. Almost everyone's here."

Julie tried to slide her hand out of Tag's. Under Joyce Marshall's cool gaze she felt as if she'd just been caught smooching with him in the living room. But he retained his firm grasp on her hand, and she couldn't pull it away without looking foolish.

Everyone turned, watching them, and Julie thought it was a miracle that she didn't stumble down the last few steps. Tag slipped his arm around her waist and guided her forward across the gleaming marble floor toward a silver-haired gentleman. Now the people began to resolve themselves into individuals, and she was surprised to see that there weren't as many as she had thought. Tag stopped in front of the older man. There was no mistaking him.

This had to be Leith Marshall, Tag's father. There, in his slender, tall frame, was Tag's lithe build, and here and there in the silvery hair were remnants of black. His eyes were blue, though paler, with an icy quality that Tag's could never have. Leith was handsome and distinguished. He was, Julie thought, just what you would think a senator or a judge or a diplomat should look like.

"Father," Tag said.

"Taggart." Leith reached out and shook his son's hand. "It's good to see you again." His eyes went to Julie, assessing her in a polite way. He smiled. "And this must be Miss Farrell."

"Julie, please." Julie was surprised she could find her voice. However smooth he might be, this man was intimidating. How had Tag managed to hold out against him all these years? But, no, that wasn't so hard to understand. There was an iron in Tag that he successfully masked with his easygoing charm.

She forced herself to hold out her hand to shake Leith's. After all, she couldn't let him think that she was some weak-kneed, frightened little creature.

"Julie. I'm honored." His grasp was firm, and his smile seemed the slightest fraction warmer. "You've met my wife already." He turned slightly toward the others, taking on the responsibility of introducing her to them. "This is Adam, our eldest son, and his lovely wife, Emily."

Adam was an older, more serious, version of Tag, though without quite the perfection of features Tag possessed. His smile was genuinely warm, as was his handshake.

But the woman beside him . . . ! Could this beautiful, poised woman with the upswept blond hair and big gray eyes possibly be the kind, sweet wallflower Tag had described? Dressed in a sleek red dress that somehow managed to be tailored, sexy and appropriate all at once, she had style and sophistication. Surely she had grown up in the same kind of exclusive atmosphere that the Marshalls had. But when she smiled, Julie could see the gentleness in her eyes and the hint of shyness.

"Hello, how are you?" Emily's voice was soft, and she gave Julie's hand a squeeze of reassurance as she shook it. "I hope we don't seem too intimidating."

"Thank you."

"Oh, Julie can take it," Tag put in cheerfully, bending down to kiss the top of her head. Julie's cheeks turned pink with embarrassment, and she avoided looking at Joyce or Leith. "She's stout-hearted. Aren't you, darling? After all, it can't be worse than sticking your head in a lion's mouth, right?"

"Stop it, Tag," Emily ordered, though her words were softened by an affectionate smile. Tag had that effect on most people, especially women. "You're embarrassing her."

"Am I?" Tag asked Julie. "I'm sorry, love."

"That's okay." Julie smiled back at him, and for a moment their eyes held. They were lost in a world all their own. They didn't see the significant glances that the other four flashed at one another, nor the small smiles of amusement and satisfaction that touched their faces.

Tag came back to the mundane world. He glanced around. "Where are the others?"

"James has not arrived yet." Joyce looked genteelly put out. "Doubtless some problems at the office. He promised me he'd be here."

"I'm sure he will," Adam assured her. "You know how irregular his hours can be. It's probably an emergency of some sort."

"Of course." Joyce barely repressed a sigh. Julie suspected that Joyce had been inconvenienced by an attorney's irregular hours a good number of times in her life. "He'll come later. Mama and Mrs. Marshall are with Aunt Caroline in the Blue Room."

The Blue Room. It had such an ostentatious ring to it, Julie thought. No doubt in this house rooms had to be identified with some color or trait; there were probably two or three living rooms, not to mention dens and rec rooms and glassed-in sun porches.

They moved together into the Blue Room, a smallish area off the formal dining room. It was wallpapered in an old-fashioned print of delicate, twining blue flowers against an eggshell-colored background, and the embroidered cushions on the antique chairs and couch were blue-flowered, as well. On the couch sat an older woman, stiff-backed and white-headed, with eyes a lighter shade of the Marshall blue. As Julie had guessed, she was introduced as Mrs. Marshall, Leith's mother. The woman beside her on the couch, younger but just as straight of back and of imperious feature, was Aunt Caroline, Leith's sister. They were exactly the type of aristocratic women Julie had expected to meet in Tag's family. His grandmother nodded coolly to her and extended her hand with the air of one granting a favor. Julie's stomach knotted up further, and she was grateful that at least Emily was there. She seemed genuinely nice beneath her attractive exterior.

Tag's mother, who was now making the introductions, expertly turned Julie from Mrs. Marshall and steered her across the room toward another woman. This woman was older, too, though her short hair was not yet entirely gray. She was short and rather pudgy, and she had a squarish face barely touched with makeup. She grinned frankly at Julie as they approached.

"Mother," Joyce said, "this is Julie, the young lady Tag brought to meet us. Julie, this is my mother, Amanda Taggart."

Mrs. Taggart reached out and pumped Julie's hand enthusiastically. "So you're the girl my boy's so excited about! I can't tell you how many times he's talked about you when he called me on the phone. I'm so happy to meet you."

"Thank you. It's nice to meet you, too," Julie replied sincerely. This woman, she knew immediately, was someone she could be friends with. "Tag told me about the summers he used to spend at your house."

"Lord, yes." Mrs. Taggart shook her head, smiling in remembrance. "He was a real corker, that boy. Always kept me on my toes. But I tell you what, I never was lonely when he was around. He's a sweetheart."

Julie flashed a look at Tag, who was standing behind her. He grinned unabashedly. "She's right." He stepped forward and gave his grandmother a healthy hug. "Hi, Gran, how're you doing?"

"Better, now that you're here." She planted an affectionate kiss on his cheek. "When are you going to make your announcement?" Her eyes twinkled up at him mischievously.

"Announcement?" Joyce turned curious eyes on her son. "Tag, what are you going to do?"

"I can't say yet. James isn't here."

"Oh, pooh!" Mrs. Taggart wrinkled her nose. "You know that boy. He may not show up 'til halfway through dinner."

But at that point the doorbell rang, and a moment later another man walked into the room. This, Julie knew immediately, had to be James. He had the family looks, though he was slightly shorter and more powerfully built. He was handsome, but there was a touch of hardness in his face that was missing in Tag's and Adam's. He was a man of power, Julie thought as he crossed the room toward them—a man who sought it, held it, used it.

"Sorry I'm late," he said as he stopped in front of his mother and bent to kiss her cheek.

"I understand, dear," Joyce Marshall told him in a tone that clearly indicated that no matter how well she understood, she didn't like it. She turned toward Julie. "Julie, I'd like you to meet Tag's other brother, James. James, this is Julie Farrell."

"Pleased to meet you." James smiled, and for a moment the charm of the Marshall men flashed in his face. His hand grasped hers firmly.

Joyce turned to Tag. "Now James is here. You can make your announcement."

Julie felt all eyes turn to her and Tag. She glanced up at him.

"Julie and I," Tag began, taking her hand, "have decided to get married."

For an instant there was a stunned silence in the room. Then everyone began to talk at once.

"Congratulations!" James reached out to shake Tag's hand, then turned to Julie. "Welcome to the family." The smile brightened his face again. "Tag seems to have gotten smarter while he's been gone."

"Thank you. I think."

The rest of the family closed in around them, offering their congratulations. Gran Taggart enveloped Julie in a big hug, and Joyce Marshall followed with a considerably more restrained kiss on the cheek. Even Leith's mother and sister left their seats on the couch and came over to give Julie their best wishes.

"This calls for a celebration," Leith Marshall declared and sent for champagne. "Julie, my dear." He took both her hands in his, and for the first time Julie saw true warmth in his face. "I can't tell you how happy I am to have you join our family." He smiled and glanced toward Emily. "Now I will have two of the prettiest women in Winston-Salem as my daughters-in-law."

"When is the wedding?" Joyce asked. "We'll need to start making plans." She began to talk of guests and churches and refreshments for the reception.

Julie felt a cold panic rising up inside her. She could just imagine a huge wedding in a strange church, surrounded by people she didn't know—and Tag's mother presiding over it all—instead of the small white frame church at home, with all her family and friends all around them. "I—uh, I'm afraid we haven't set a date yet," she stammered.

"Oh." Mrs. Marshall looked nonplussed. "I see. Well, it's never too early to start thinking about these things."

Tag grimaced. "Mother, please, you'll scare her to death. Actually, I think we would probably like to have a rather small wedding."

"A small wedding?" Joyce's face registered cool disbelief. "Oh . . . well . . . there's plenty of time to discuss it."

Julie had the feeling the subject was far from closed. Tag's mother was going to want a big wedding, and she would want it in Winston-Salem, too, not some little town in Texas where none of her society friends would go. But Julie decided there was no way she was going to let Joyce Marshall run her wedding. What a terrible way to start off with Tag's family—getting into a fight with his mother over the wedding plans!

The champagne arrived, and Leith toasted the engaged couple. Then they moved into the dining room, where a long table had been set elegantly. Silver, china and crystal gleamed in the sparkling light from the cut glass chandelier above. Julie didn't think she had ever seen so many utensils, glasses and plates at one setting before in her life. What were they supposed to do with all of them?

They sat down, and a uniformed waiter brought out the first course. The talk drifted away from the wedding and on to legal cases and various people Tag and the others all knew. With each passing minute Julie felt more and more removed from the place and the people. Though the others made a polite effort to include her in their conversation, she didn't know the people they were talking about and, frankly, wasn't interested in them, anyway.

After the meal the party split up, with Joyce leading the women into the sitting room where they had been earlier and the Marshall men remaining in the dining room. Julie glanced back as she strolled down the hall beside Emily, surprised to see that neither Tag nor any of the other men was going with them. It reminded her of something out of a novel about Victorian England! Did people really still do this—the women retiring by themselves, leaving the men to an after-dinner cigar and a brandy?

Emily, noticing Julie's amazed expression, giggled softly and leaned closer to her to murmur, "It's a Marshall family tradition, I think. The men are always going off to confab about something or other. I think it comes from their working together. Or maybe it's because Leith used to smoke like a chimney, and Joyce can't stand smoke. Anyway, I don't think I've ever been to a Marshall family dinner where the men didn't wind up in the library together after the meal. Pretty Gothic, huh?"

Julie nodded slowly. The low-burning panic that had sprung to life when Tag's mother started talking wedding plans flared up again. Was she going to spend the rest of her life in this town with these people? Going to dinner parties at the Marshall house and being shunted off into the women's section after dinner while Tag talked to his father and brothers? Was Tag going to change and become like this? Would he no longer be the same easygoing, blue-jeaned man she knew, always ready to laugh or talk, comfortable sitting with her family around the kitchen table or working in the barn at the B & K?

Winston-Salem and North Carolina were beautiful; she had to give them that. But how was she going to live here? How could she stand to leave the place and people she loved to live in a house that was more like a museum than a home, surrounded by coolly elegant people like Joyce and Leith Marshall? When she had told Tag that she would marry him, she had thought she loved him enough to take anything, but now she was beginning to wonder if "anything" would slowly smother that love.

Julie sneaked a glance at Emily. She seemed happy enough living this way. Maybe it was something you got used to. Maybe she would find out it wasn't all that bad. Still, she couldn't quiet the niggling little doubt inside her. What if she found out that it *was* just as bad as she imagined?

Chapter 11

"Well, Tag." Leith clapped his son's shoulder in an unaccustomed gesture of affection. All four of the Marshall men had drifted into the library, which was Leith's personal retreat. Leith poured them each a brandy. "So you're finally going to settle down. You know how glad I am to hear it."

"I know."

"She seems like a nice girl," Leith went on, automatically going around behind his desk to sit down.

"Very attractive," Adam commented, settling into one of the comfortable leather chairs. Tag flopped into another chair, casually hooking one leg over the arm. James took the corner of his father's desk, half sitting, half leaning against it, braced by one extended leg.

"Not your type, I would have thought," Leith remarked. "She's not like any of the other girls you've dated."

Tag grinned. "Ah, but I never fell for any of them."

Leith smiled faintly. "True." He paused, studying his brandy as he slowly swirled it around the snifter. "The thing is, Tag, how happy do you think she's going to be here? She doesn't strike me as being accustomed to the sort of life you lead. I can't see her at the Snowflake Ball or heading up a charity drive."

"Thank God," James commented sotto voce.

Leith cast James a dry look. "We all know your feelings on the matter, James. I don't think they are to the point. The issue is whether Miss Farrell is up to assuming the position that she will naturally be expected—"

James made a theatrical groan and stood up from the edge of the desk. "*Expected* be damned! I doubt that anyone will expect a thing from her except you. Really, Father, couldn't you lay off him for once? I mean, he's getting married—to, I might add, a remarkably nice, pleasant young woman—which is what you've been wanting him to do for years. Why can't you leave it at that? Why do you have to decide now that his future wife should be a certain kind of woman?"

Tag stared at James in amazement. Was James actually standing up for him? James had always been more likely to agree with his father that Tag was wasting his life.

"I am not deciding!" Leith snapped. "I was merely asking Tag a question. I was concerned about his wife's happiness—and his, too."

"Wait, wait." Tag lifted his hands. "There's no need to get in an argument over this. It's a moot point. It doesn't matter whether Julie could take being a Marshall and a Taggart in Winston-Salem. We won't be living here."

All three of the other men swiveled their heads to stare at him. "What?" Leith's voice was stunned.

"You're going to stay in Texas?" Adam asked.

Tag nodded. "Yes. You see, I didn't only find Julie there. I found something I want to do."

"You want to live on a ranch?"

"I don't just want to live there. I've been working there, too, and I enjoy it. It's something I like. Mike's been teaching me the business, and I've read up on it. It's interesting. I haven't had a chance to discuss it with Julie yet, but that won't be a problem. She'll love it."

"My God," Leith said in a tone of deep wonder.

"But that's not all. I want to expand the operation. That's one reason why I came home this weekend. I wanted to talk to you about it."

Leith continued to simply look at Tag. James and Adam exchanged an amused glance. The look on their father's face was priceless.

Tag went on, "I want to raise horses, too. I enjoyed working the B and K, but I realize I'd enjoy it even more if we bred horses, not just cattle. Besides, I have quite a bit more expertise with horses. I'm not talking about anything huge at first, but it will mean some expenditure—a horse barn, a few fences, equipment, salaries. I'll need to hire an expert to manage that side of it. I've put together some figures."

He pulled out a couple of sheets of paper from inside his suit jacket and unfolded them, laying them down on the desk in front of his father. Leith looked even more amazed, if that were possible, but he picked up a pair of glasses from his desk and put them on to study the figures. Tag stood beside him and explained the projected costs.

"What I was thinking of was leasing the house and part of the land from you, just enough for the horse farm. I'd put up the improvements, of course, as long as it was a long-term lease. I've already been talking to a bank in Texas about a loan for the capital outlay."

"I hardly know what to say." A little smile quirked the corners of Leith's mouth. "Tag, I would have said that nothing you could do would surprise me, but I must admit, you've really floored me this time." He looked at his son for a moment, then decisively nodded his head. "All right. I'll talk to our tax and contracts attorneys on Monday. I'm sure we'll be able to work something out." He rose and held out his hand. Tag shook it.

They remained for a few more minutes in the study, but the conversation dragged. After Tag's bombshell, anything else seemed rather anticlimactic. Before long they decided to rejoin the women in the Blue Room. Adam and his father walked out, idly discussing a problem in the firm, but James lingered behind.

"Tag..."

Tag turned on his way to the door and looked back at James questioningly. "Yeah?"

"I was..." Being James, he chose his words carefully, "...rather taken aback to see how surprised you were when I told Leith to lay off you."

Tag shrugged. "Well, let's just say it's not your usual stance."

"Am I that hard on you? No. Don't answer that. I hope you realize that I've never been *against* you."

"I know. You simply hate to see waste."

"That's true. But I've always wanted to see you happy. I thought I had the answer to that. Anyway, I can see that you're happy now, and I'm glad. I wanted you to know that."

Tag smiled. "Thanks."

James pushed himself away from the wall where he had been leaning and started across the room. "You know, Leith's right about one thing. You have changed."

"Maybe. I can't see it." Tag hesitated, then went on, "I think you're the one who's changed."

"What do you mean?" James glanced at him, surprised. "Because I stood up for you?"

"Not only that. There's—I don't know—something different about you."

James smile was wry and contained little amusement. "Just a few complications in my life."

"Romantic?" Tag guessed.

James sighed. "Have you ever wanted someone, more than wanted her, maybe even loved her, and been certain there was no hope for you?"

"No." Tag shook his head. Concern shadowed his face. "James, what is it? Have you gotten tangled up with a married woman?"

"No. Worse, probably. Someone involved in a case I worked on."

"Oh. On the other side?"

"Yeah. That's why I said there was no hope." There was a moment of silence; then James forced a smile onto his face. "But, hey, what're we talking about that for? We should be talking about you and your fiancée." He started briskly out the door. "So tell me, how did all this come about?"

Tag frowned. He hated to drop the subject with James still so obviously troubled by it. But he knew that there was no getting James to tell you something if he didn't want to. This was one story James wasn't about to divulge. He followed his brother out the door, telling him comically about the first time he met Julie. But when they neared the room where the rest of the family were waiting, Tag took James's arm and pulled him to a stop.

"You know," he said in a low, earnest voice, "if you ever need to tell anybody about it . . ."

James flashed a grin. "Me? The prosecuting attorney without a heart? Nah."

"James . . ."

"Okay, okay. Sure. You'll be the first to know. After all, we're brothers, right?"

"Right." Tag smiled, and they went into the room together.

Julie spent a restless night, waking often, plagued by confused dreams. In one she was on her way to church to marry Tag but she couldn't find her car, so she had to walk. A Cadillac pulled up and offered her a ride, and when she looked in, she saw her father was driving it, her mother on the seat beside him. Overjoyed to see them, she hopped in the car, and it took off. She felt very happy with them, warm and light, but gradually she began to grow uneasy, and then she realized that they were driving *away* from the wedding instead of toward it. She pointed out the mistake, but her mother said that she thought Julie would like to spend some time with them. Julie protested that she would, but Tag was waiting for her. Still they kept going in the wrong direction. Julie tried and tried to tell them to turn around, but she could never get the words out right or something would happen to cut her off. And all the while they drove farther and farther away.

She woke up from the dream in a sweat, her heart pounding. She was scared and empty, as if she actually *had* lost Tag. She wanted to cry. It had been a long time since either one of her parents had appeared in her dreams, and she hated the fact that they had been in one that had left her with such a bad feeling. She lay awake almost until morning, reluctant to go back to sleep.

When at last she did fall asleep, it was for far too short a time, and she awoke feeling tired and heavy-eyed. But it was impossible to remain that way for long with Tag around. He was full of good spirits, and by her second cup of coffee he had coaxed her into a pleasant mood, as well. After she had eaten he insisted that they go on a shopping expedition.

The first stop was a jewelry store. Julie looked at him in confusion. "I thought we were going to find a dress for tonight?"

"We are. But first—" He jumped out of the car and came around to open her door.

"But first what?"

"First things, of course. How can I go around announcing our engagement to everyone if you aren't even wearing a ring?"

"A ring?" Julie looked at him blankly. She hadn't even thought about a ring. "An engagement ring?"

"Sure." He pulled her to him for a quick kiss, then stood smiling down into her eyes. "You ready?"

A curious blend of excitement and fear rose in her. She nodded, and they went inside. It was an elegant, quiet store, with thick carpets and glistening glass cases and dangling chandeliers. The manager came over to help them personally. He pulled out a tray for them to look at more closely. Julie was dazzled by the row upon row of blazing diamond rings. She couldn't choose among them. They all looked tremendously big and expensive.

"I don't know." She felt a little nervous and inadequate to choose among such things. She turned to Tag. "Which one do you like?" He obviously fit in here; he knew what to do, unlike her.

He picked out three or four, and she tried them on.

"I like this one." Tag held one up. "What do you think?"

"It's beautiful." She tried it on again, holding out her hand and turning it this way and that. The diamond caught the light and flashed. She tried to imagine lifting and loading feed sacks with that ring sparkling on her finger. It was a ludicrous image.

Tag placed his hand under hers, holding her hand up as he looked at the ring. "It's beautiful on you."

He lifted her hand to his mouth and softly kissed the back of it. Julie looked up at him, and the love she felt for him washed through her anew.

"Is this the one you want?" he asked. She nodded. Frankly, she didn't care. But it was the one Tag wanted to give her.

He bought the ring, and she wore it out of the store. She sat looking at it as they drove away. It was lovely, but it felt uncomfortable and heavy on her finger. Somehow, seeing it on her hand made the wedding seem much more real and final.

Next he took her to an elegant boutique, where she tried on one evening gown after another. All of them were beautiful, and each one had a price tag that made her cringe. She had a difficult time choosing between two of them, so Tag decided that he would simply get both.

"After all," he reasoned, "you can wear the other one some other time."

Julie started to ask him exactly where he thought she could wear the floor-length beaded dress. To the next dance at the local dance hall? But then she remembered that they would be coming back here to live. She would have plenty of opportunities to wear it. The thought depressed her spirits.

Once Tag had purchased the dresses they had lunch in the open air café in the atrium of a downtown hotel. All through the meal Julie kept feeling his eyes on her. She would glance up to find that he was watching her with that heavy-lidded gaze that she had come to know meant he desired her. He had looked at her that way while she was modeling the dresses, too. Julie smiled to herself. She rather liked knowing that he wanted her. In fact, the glow in his eyes started a hot, melting sensation in her own abdomen.

The only problem was, what were they going to do about it? She simply could not make love in that museum of a house his parents owned, particularly with his mother and the housekeeper and who knew who else around. And Tag had sublet his condominium; that was the reason they were staying with his parents in the first place.

Somehow the realization that they could not consummate the passion beginning to well inside them merely increased their desire. Julie couldn't stop blatantly sexual images from coming to her mind, and she knew from the slight widening of Tag's eyes that he had guessed where her thoughts lay.

Suddenly everything they did seemed tinged with sexuality. She watched him bite into his sandwich, saw the sharp, white gleam of his teeth, and all she could think of was the nip of his teeth upon her neck. She lifted up a black olive from her salad and slowly put it in her mouth, her lips pursing around it, lingering on the smooth surface. Tag's eyes went to her mouth, and his gaze darkened. Julie chose another olive and, picking it up with her fingers, held it out to Tag. He leaned forward, and his teeth closed around the morsel, taking it straight from her hand. His lips brushed against her fingertips, soft and lingering. A ball of fire seemed to drop straight down and burst in her abdomen, sending shivers all through her.

Their lunch lay forgotten on their plates as they looked at each other. Julie could see the desire written plainly on Tag's face, feel its pulse beating deep within her own body. Her breasts were aching for his touch, her whole body humming with frustrated passion. His gaze traveled down her face, touched her breasts, then moved lower until the table blocked his view. His eyes came back up slowly. Julie's skin felt on fire everywhere his eyes had touched, as though it had been his fingertips roving her body.

Tag stood up abruptly and tossed down the money to pay for their meal. Then he took her hand and led her quickly from the restaurant. Without pausing, he walked straight across the lobby to the registration desk. Julie watched in amazement as he tossed a credit card down on the counter and began to register. He was actually getting a room just so they could—

She glanced around, feeling heat rising in her face. What must the desk clerk think of them, registering in the middle of the day without a single article of luggage anywhere about them? He would have to know why they were renting the room. It was embarrassing. But there was a certain titillation in it, too. It seemed positively wicked and illicit, and somehow that made what they were doing even more exciting.

Tag pocketed the key and took her hand again without a word, walking her over to the bank of elevators. They looked at each other as they waited for the elevator to come, but there was such heat and intensity in their eyes that they had to look away after a moment. Otherwise, Julie thought, they might start kissing right there in the lobby, and if that happened, she didn't know where it would stop. The glass-walled elevator came at last, and they stepped inside, carefully standing on opposite sides. They shot up. Tension lay in the space between them, almost tangible, like a cord holding them together, yet pushing them apart at the same time. Julie wished the glass walls of the elevator didn't open onto the lobby; otherwise, they would already be in each other's arms.

Their room was at the far end of the hall. Even the long walk aroused Julie. She was supremely conscious of Tag's body beside her, slender and hard. Of his muscles, his flesh, the shape and texture of him. She could almost taste his skin upon her lips. They halted in front of the door to the room, and Tag slid the key into the lock. His fingers trembled slightly, and he had to try a second time to fit it in. He turned the key and opened the door, turning as he did so to take Julie's arm and pull her inside with him.

She leaped into his arms, and the door sighed shut behind them. Their lips met and clung. Tag's breath shuddered out as his lips dug into hers and his tongue delved into her mouth. His hands slid firmly down her body, rediscovering the gentle curves, and cupped her buttocks. His fingertips dug in, lifting her into him so that they were pressed together tightly. Julie could feel every hard line of his body against her own softer flesh. She moaned a little and moved against him. His response was to shift his mouth and kiss her even more deeply. His hands, grasping her hips, rubbed her mound suggestively against his own hard flesh.

He walked her backward toward the bed, kissing her again and again. They fell onto the mattress and rolled across it in a frenzy of kissing and caressing. They tore at their clothing, unable to stay apart long enough to completely undress. Instead they disrobed in bits and pieces between and around kisses, tossing their garments aside until at last there was nothing between them save the clinging of flesh to warm flesh, hungry and vital.

Tag's mouth moved down her in a long, slow journey of arousal. He kissed her skin, teasing with his tongue and gently nibbling with his lips, spending what seemed an eon on her breasts until she was twisting and moaning beneath him, begging for release. Then his lips trailed downwards, off the plateau of her ribcage and over the soft plane of her belly, going farther and farther down until at last he found the prize he sought.

Julie let out a gasp as his mouth gently laved the tiny, pulsing nub at the center of her desire. His hands went beneath her, lifting her up to his questing mouth. She groaned, her fingers digging frantically into the bedspread beneath her. The wave of passion building in her crested and broke, washing out through her body.

She lay trembling. Drained and blissful, the tiny aftershocks of pleasure still running through her. But then he moved into her, deeply, slowly, and desire began to rise in her again. His movements quickened until he was thrusting fast and hard, and then they crashed together through the invisible barrier into a searing, shattering oneness.

They collapsed together, shaken by the strength of their feelings. For the moment all thoughts of the ring or the wedding or Tag's family had flown, and Julie was aware of nothing but a peaceful, glorious contentment.

Sighing, she kissed his shoulder and murmured, "I love you."

*   *   *

Julie opened her eyes and looked out the window. They were getting close to home. Only another five miles. She smiled. It would be wonderful to get back. She wanted to know how her family was, how the store had done, whether the football team had won their first play-off game.

She glanced across the car at Tag. He felt her gaze and looked at her, then smiled. "Just wake up?"

"Yeah." She nodded. She was swept by a wave of guilt. She loved Tag so much. She had hoped, really hoped, that she would like North Carolina enough that she would be happy to live there. Instead she had come home full of doubts. It was a beautiful place. Many of the people she had met were nice. She liked Tag's brothers and Emily. She liked Mrs. Taggart. Even his parents hadn't been that bad, when you got right down to it. They were pleasant and polite, and they had actually seemed pleased to hear that Tag was going to marry her.

It was just that she didn't fit. She had felt like a fish out of water half the time. And the party last night had proved it. The club had been beautifully decorated and filled with well-dressed people. Tag had introduced her to scores of men and women, most of whose names she could not remember. All of them had been polite to her, but there was no mistaking the fact that she was an outsider. She didn't know any of the people or events they talked about. Everyone seemed so glittering and glamorous, the women all perfectly coiffed and dressed in gowns that cost more than her store often made in profit in a month. Even though she knew that her evening gown was as beautiful and expensive as any of theirs, she had felt out of place. After all, she didn't really belong in a dress like the one she'd worn. She didn't *belong* there. And she was sure that she must have stuck out like a sore thumb.

Tag, on the other hand, was right at home. He belonged here; she could see that more with each passing moment. He laughed and joked and seemed to be having the time of his life. It made her wonder miserably how long he could be happy with someone as simple and ordinary as she was. Surely someday he would want something—someone!—more.

Marilyn, the woman who had come to visit Tag in Texas, had been there, and *she* had fit in. She had also made it a point not to talk to either Tag or Julie all evening, which hadn't made Julie unhappy. However, a woman Julie would have sworn everyone called "Pokey" and who was practically a clone of Marilyn, did bend Julie's ear for about fifteen minutes, relating various juicy bits of gossip concerning Tag's past love affairs with several of the women in the room.

Her spite had been so obvious that Julie had found it easy to avoid being jealous over the stories. But she had realized, with a sinking heart, that she would probably have to put up with a great deal of this sort of talk when she married Tag. There were, no doubt, many women who would resent an interloper like herself coming in and snapping up one of the most eligible bachelors in the city. She was sure she would have to face all kinds of subtle digs and veiled insults. There would surely be talk all over town about the faux pas she made or any outfit she wore that wasn't quite right. She had never before realized how much, by marrying Tag, she would be put on display.

By the time the evening was over the wonderful glow she had felt from the afternoon had vanished. She had gone to bed feeling depressed, and this morning when she woke up she had been little better.

Julie looked down at her hand lying in her lap. The diamond ring caught the sun and flashed brilliantly. It felt heavy on her finger, as if it weighed her down.

Tag zipped through town and turned onto the road leading to Julie's house. Within minutes they were there. As soon as his car stopped in the driveway, the front door banged open, and Cathy rushed out to meet them. On her heels were all the dogs, yapping and jumping and wagging their tails in joy as if Julie had been absent for a month instead of just three days.

"Did you have fun?" Cathy bubbled, not giving her sister a chance to answer. "Is their house gorgeous? Oh! Look at that diamond!" She took Julie's hand and held it up. "Wow!"

Riley came out of the house more slowly and gave Julie a one-armed hug. "Hey, Jule. Say, did you go somewhere?" he teased.

Julie gave him a poke in the ribs. "Very funny." She glanced around. "Where's Granddad? The truck's here."

"He's down burning off the front pasture." Burning off a pasture was a common practice. It got rid of the leaves, seeds and general trash that accumulated over time and left a layer of potash, which would feed the soil.

"Oh. Well, maybe I'll run down there after a while and say hi to him."

They all went inside the house, congregating as usual in the kitchen. Julie laid out a snack and drinks while they exchanged information about their respective weekends. She and Tag related all the high points of their visit, and Cathy responded with the news from home.

When they had finished eating Julie decided to take a drink and a sandwich down to her grandfather. Tag and Cathy walked with her down the path by the animal pens to the front pasture. They found Horace standing by the fence, keeping a careful eye on his fire.

"Hey, darlin'," he called when he spotted Julie and walked over to her, his arms outspread.

"Hi, Granddad." Julie hugged him, then handed him the sack lunch they'd brought him. "Thought you might like some sustenance."

"Say, this is great." Horace dug into the sack and pulled out of can of soda.

They stood for a while, chatting with Horace and watching the fire. Horace had disked around three sides of the portion of the pasture he was burning off so as to contain the blaze. The fourth side was a strip of boggy land, a natural fire break.

"Wind's starting to change on me," Horace said in disgust. "It was coming from the west, but now it's shifted out of the southwest. Picking up, too."

They could see that in the flames, which were turning in a more northerly direction toward the boggy strip and flaring higher, fanned by the wind. As they watched the fire burned closer to the marshy area.

Horace frowned. "I ought to set a backfire."

Just as he spoke a gust of wind hit the fire and it leaped across the open space of wet land. Suddenly the dry grass on the other side was aflame. Horace dropped his soft drink, cursing eloquently, and started running for the new fire. Julie ran, too, quickly outstripping the older man, with Tag and Cathy right on her heels.

Tag had never seen a pasture burned off before, but it was obvious what was wrong. The fire had leaped out of its bounds and was now eating its way freely across the fields and stands of trees. Even more frightening was the fact that the fire was travelling in the direction of the Farrell house.

As she ran, Julie glanced around for something she could use to beat out the flames. She stopped and yanked up a small cedar bush, then charged up to the fire and began beating at its edge. The others followed her lead, but they were forced steadily back by the wind-fed blaze. The fire flamed high and hot, crackling swiftly across the grass and brush.

"Cathy!" Julie turned to her sister. "Run back to the house and call the fire department! Then you and Riley get the hoses and start watering down the house and everything around it. Get the animals out of the pen."

Cathy's eyes widened. "You think it'll get that far?"

"There's nothing to stop it." Julie looked expressively at the fire, already twice as large as it had been despite their efforts to stop it.

Cathy took off at a run. The other three continued to beat at the flames. Julie's arms grew tired, but she continued to swing the small bush. It, too, finally caught on fire, and she threw it to the ground and stamped it out, then ran to pull up another one. She turned and started back, glancing across at Tag as she did.

Tag and Horace had spread out across the line of the fire, which had bulged northward so that flames now burned between Julie and the men. As she watched, the fire popped, and a shower of sparks flew out, landing in a vague semicircle behind Tag. Instantly the grass and weeds flamed up.

Tag was trapped in the middle of the fire!

For an instant Julie froze in horror, her heart plunging downward. She couldn't breathe, couldn't move, couldn't think. Then she broke from her momentary paralysis and ran toward him, screaming, "Tag! Tag!"

Horace, hearing her yell, glanced at Tag and saw the problem. He reached him before Julie did and began flailing away at the new flames, as Tag did on the other side. Between the two of them they cleared a path, and Tag ran out. Julie dropped the cedar bush she'd been holding and launched herself straight at Tag, wrapping her arms around him and holding on tightly.

"Hey, sweetheart, it's all right." He folded her in his arms soothingly. "I'm okay."

"Come on, you two," Horace called.

He was right, Julie knew. They had too much to do for her to give in to her fear. She forced herself to step back from Tag and pick up the bush again. But she was trembling all over as she worked, and it wasn't from exhaustion. She kept thinking of that moment of sheer, icy terror when she had seen Tag engulfed by the flames and thought she was about to see him die right before her eyes.

The fire swept on, pushing them backward. They were getting close to the stand of trees right before the animal pens, and Julie knew that it would all be over if the fire started on the trees.

A pickup truck screeched to a halt on the highway outside the fence, then backed up and pulled off the road. Two husky men in ball caps rushed to the fence. "You folks need help?" one called. It was a rhetorical question, for he was already climbing over the fence and loping toward them. The other one was busy pulling out blankets and a fire extinguisher from the cab of the truck. Then he ran after his companion.

"We're with the Cherry Grove Volunteer Fire Department," the first one said, naming a tiny town a few miles south of them. "Darrell called 'em on the CB when we saw ya'll."

He handed a blanket to Horace and kept the other one, attacking the fire with certain glee. Julie suspected that the Cherry Grove Volunteer Fire Department didn't get a lot of calls. This was probably the most excitement Darrell and his companion had had in months.

The high-pitched whine of a siren split the air, and Julie sagged with relief. The Brinkman Fire Department was coming. A few minutes later the small fire truck, bought several years ago from a larger city where it was deemed obsolete, came trundling toward them, east of the fire. Obviously the driver had struck out on his own instead of following Riley's and Cathy's directions, for he was on a trail that looked good close to the house but which quickly petered out and dropped down to a small gully.

Horace and Julie began to yell, motioning to the firemen to come back and try another way. The two men on the back of the truck waved back cheerfully at them, and the truck rumbled on down to the gully and began to cross it. The truck lurched to a stop as its front wheels started up the other side. The driver gunned the motor. The wheels spun. The truck rocked and went nowhere.

"Well, I'll be damned!" Horace said, sweeping his hat off his head and throwing it to the ground in disgust. "If that isn't just like Billy Sneed! He always thinks he knows where he's going, and he can hardly find his way home."

They turned back to beating at the fire while the firemen tried in vain to get the truck unstuck. Julie's arms were so tired she thought they would fall off. From across the field behind them she could hear the firemen shouting at each other.

A horn tooted merrily on the highway, and they looked up. There sat a pickup truck with a large water tank mounted on the back. Across the side of the tank was the lettering Cherry Grove Fire Department.

"Hey, Darrell! John!" A man leaned out the passenger window of the truck. "We're here! Where do we get in?"

"Take down the damned fence," Horace growled.

"Sure. I got a pair of wire cutters in my truck," volunteered Darrell, who seemed to be prepared for any emergency.

Within minutes a section of the fence was down and the pickup rattled across the field. The men trained their hose on the fire, sweeping up and down, and the flames stopped their advance.

But it was a standoff. They weren't pushing the fire back. And it was obvious that the water supply was limited. Julie, Tag and Horace stood watching, dirty and blackened with smoke, while the battle went on between the volunteers in their baseball caps and blue jeans and the roaring fire.

Then suddenly, miraculously, the wind shifted again. Now the flames bent back toward the firebreak, and the water, beating at its tail end, gradually doused the fire. The only flames left were a few small ones burning at the other edge of the firebreak. Within minutes, as quickly as it had started, the danger was over.

Julie sagged with relief. Her arms felt like lead and the adrenaline had seeped away, leaving her weak and tired. The house was out of danger. The pens. The barn. The sheds. Tears filled her eyes.

Outside the fence a tow truck roared to a stop. The driver leaned out. "You the guys who need a fire truck pulled out?" he asked, disbelief tingeing his voice.

Horace jerked a thumb toward the beached truck in the gully. The driver couldn't suppress a grin. "Well, I'll be."

Julie glanced at Tag. His blue eyes, startlingly light in his smudged face, glittered with amusement. She began to laugh. It set Tag off, too, and in a moment they were sitting together on the ground, holding their sides and gasping with laughter.

Long after their hysterical laughter had subsided, long after all the trucks and firefighters had gone and Tag had returned home and Julie had spent considerable time in the shower scrubbing away the afternoon's grime, she sat in her bedroom in the old rocker, looking out the window and thinking. At first her mind lingered on that moment when Tag had been in danger and everything inside her had gone numb with fear, but resolutely she pushed it to the back of her brain. Instead she thought about the weekend that had just passed, about Tag's parents and the dance at the club, about the people she had met and the way they lived, the way she would live from now on.

And she knew she couldn't do it. She was who she was, and she couldn't change. Not even for Tag.

Julie had never been one to skirt an issue or to take the easy way out. Once she had made up her mind— and had cried more than a little over it—she resolutely got up and drove over to Tag's house. It was late, but a light was still on in his window. Even if it hadn't been, Julie would have awakened him. She had to do what she had to do. Now. Before she lost her nerve.

Tag answered the door, his face creasing into a pleased grin when he saw her. "Julie! Come on in." He reached out and took her arm, pulling her inside and bending to kiss her.

She sidestepped the kiss. She couldn't take that now. She might break down and begin to cry before she said what she had to say.

Tag looked at her, puzzled. "Julie? What's the matter?"

"I need to talk to you." She straightened, looking him in the eye.

"All right. Let's go into the den."

She followed him down the hall to the small, comfortable room. He sat down, but she remained standing. She couldn't sit still. She began to pace.

Tag, feeling awkward, rose to face her. "Julie, what is it?"

She took a breath. "I've come to return this." She pulled the engagement ring off her finger and held it out to him.

Tag looked at it blankly. "The ring?"

"Yes. I—I can't marry you."

He looked stunned. "You what?"

"I can't marry you. I—it wouldn't be fair to either one of us."

"What the hell are you talking about?"

"I realized it this weekend. When we were at your parents' house. It's something I've always known, but I didn't want to admit it. We're too different. There's no way we can make a marriage work. I thought I could change, that I could make myself fit into your world, but I know now that I can't. We're light years apart. When I met your mother and all those other women, and I saw how they acted and what they did and where they lived, well, I knew then that I could never be like them. I don't want to be like them."

"I don't want you to be like them, either!" Tag exclaimed. "I've been around women like that all my life, and I never wanted to marry any of them. You're the only woman I want to marry. *You* are who I want."

"I've been thinking about that. I haven't been able to understand what it is you see in me. There are so many women who are prettier, smarter, funnier than I am. Women who know how to dress and how to look. But I realized that it must be rebellion. You're always fighting your parents and the whole system that you come from. I'm the opposite of that, and by marrying me, you're defying them again.''

''What a crock,'' Tag said scornfully, reaching out to grasp her shoulders. ''Do you actually believe what you're saying? It is not rebellion. I'm not a teenager anymore. I am not defying my parents. *I love you!*''

''You love me precisely because I'm so utterly wrong for you. That's the biggest part of my appeal for you.''

Tag groaned. ''Julie, this is the craziest thing I've ever heard. What's gotten into you? Why this switch? This morning everything was fine. Now here you are telling me that we're wrong for each other and can't get married.''

''No, it wasn't fine this morning. Not inside me. Tag, right now you may not care that I'm not like the women you're used to. But as we get older, it will make a big difference. You'll expect me to fit into the mold, and I can't. After you're married things change. People want it to be the way they're used to. I'll never fit into your family. I'll never fit into your group of friends. And what's more, I don't want to! I didn't like going to that dance. I didn't enjoy the formal dinner at your parents' house. I don't want to move to Winston-Salem and have your mother show me the ropes of society. I don't—''

''Whoa. Wait a minute. Move? Who said anything about moving to Winston-Salem?''

''Well, nobody,'' she admitted. ''But you'll want to go home sometime.''

"Maybe for a visit. You think you can't stand it for a week or so every now and then?"

"Well, of course I can. It's not that I can't stand it."

"Then what is it?"

Momentary confusion swept her. "Are you saying you want to stay here?"

"Well, of course. Why did you think I told you all about the horse farm? Just to hear myself talk?"

"No. But I assumed you would hire someone to run it locally and you would be, you know, sort of over-seeing it from your home."

"I will be. From my home right here." He pointed down at the floor. "Did you honestly think I was going to jerk you up and cart you off to North Carolina?" He shook his head. "Julie, sweetheart, don't you know me better than that? I never had a real home. A place that was home in my heart, I mean, until I met you. You're my home, my family. I would never, ever ask you to leave this place. You have roots that go deep—I know you'd wilt away from here. I wouldn't demand that of you. Besides, I like it here. I want to live here."

"Really?" Tears sprang into her eyes, and she felt the warmth of his love spreading through her. She wanted to throw her arms around him and feel him holding her, but she bit her lip and made herself take a step back. "But that's not all. It isn't simply that I don't want to move. It's—it's everything. We're wrong for each other. We don't fit."

Tag shoved his fingers deep into his hair. "I feel like I'm in some crazy dream where nothing makes sense, but it keeps going on anyway. Julie, I love you. You love me. What could be wrong in that?"

"If you think about it, you'll understand."

"I won't. I don't. It's ridiculous."

"No! It's the truth! If we got married, you'd begin to resent me for all the things you've had to give up. You'd wish I acted the way those other women act. You'd want to go back to the things you enjoy, the life you like. And I'm not cut out for it! I can't give little parties and serve itty bitty sandwiches with the crusts cut off. I don't want to go to the ballet or the opera, or a charity ball or a dance at the country club. It's not me!"

"I realize that."

"But it *is* you. That's what you've always known, and you'll miss it. After a while, you'll miss it."

"Don't you think you're taking an awful lot of responsibility on yourself?" His voice was tight and angry, his brows drawn together. "Deciding what I really want, what will be best for me, what I ought to do. Those are things that only I know! And I'm telling you, none of that is true!"

"You just don't realize it!" Tag made a frustrated noise, and she went on hurriedly. "Trust me. I know I'm right. If we get married, you'll regret it. In a few years you'll understand what a big mistake it was, but by then it'll be too late. You'll want to get out, and it will break my heart!"

"What do you think you're doing to mine right now?"

"Don't say that!" she whispered.

"Why not? It's true. What am I supposed to do? Pretend that I don't feel anything so you can get away clean? Protect you from your guilt? Well, dammit, you should feel guilty. I hope you feel guilty as hell!

What have you been doing, stringing me along all this time? And now you've decided you can't go through with it? Or maybe you never intended to go through with it. Maybe you only wanted to see if you could catch me. Is that it?''

"No!" His words stung. "No, Tag, I never tried to string you along. I love you!"

"You have a hell of a way of showing it, then."

"Tag, this is for the best."

"Right." He gave her a blank, cold look that reminded her shiveringly of his father.

She wanted to tell him that he would get over the hurt, that someday he would realize that she had acted for the best, but the words stuck in her throat. With a choked cry, she ran from the room, leaving him behind her.

Chapter 12

Julie dragged through the days that followed. She tried to fill them up with work and her family, but there didn't seem to be enough of either one to get rid of all the gaps in her life. What had she done before she met Tag? She tried to remember, but it seemed an eon ago.

Work was often boring and it was a tremendous effort to chat with the customers. She didn't want to talk; she didn't want to listen to their jokes. She wanted to curl up in a corner and cry. She felt lost and empty without Tag. She had never dreamed it would be this hard to live without him.

At home Cathy was angry at Julie because she had broken her engagement to Tag. Cathy liked Tag and thought he would make a super brother-in-law. She couldn't understand why Julie had sent him away, and on one occasion when Julie tried to explain, Cathy had ended up declaring disgustedly, "You're nuts," and walked away.

Even if Cathy hadn't been mad at Julie, she wouldn't have been any company. The younger woman was more and more involved with her friends, basketball practice and her FFA projects. Nor was Riley around much. When he wasn't locked up in his room, he was out with his girlfriend or hanging around the Kustard Korner with his friends. Lyle was gone almost all the time, what with his job and college. Even Granddad was rarely home. He was usually out with Riette. Of course, that was nothing new, but it contributed to the empty atmosphere of the house.

Julie cried about the fact that she was losing her family. She cried about everything these days. Once she broke off a fingernail lifting a bag of feed and burst into tears, then had to climb into the loft and sit by herself until she'd regained control.

In the same way that she couldn't seem to control her tears, she also had trouble controlling her thoughts. A dozen times a day they turned to Tag. At first he phoned her often, but she refused to talk to him. He also came by the house a couple of times, but she didn't answer the door. Finally he stopped trying to contact her.

After that it seemed she thought about him even more. She wondered where he was and what he was doing. Was he still at the ranch? Had he flown back to North Carolina? Once she saw his car in front of the post office and her heart positively leaped in her chest. She drove by slowly, both hoping and fearing that he would emerge so that she could catch a glimpse of him.

She went over all the things they'd done together, remembering what Tag had said and done, how he had looked at this time or that, how he had laughed or smiled or frowned. No one else could wink quite like him, with those beautiful thick-lashed eyes, or convey such sardonic astonishment with only a raised eyebrow. She even recalled silly jokes he had told and would start laughing, only to end up crying. She missed his kisses and caresses, his bone-melting love-making. She simply missed his presence, the warm reassurance of his lean body and quick mind.

Even the coming of Christmas couldn't bring her out of her doldrums. In the past Julie had loved the holiday, happily buying gifts for her brothers and sisters and secreting them away. She would spend her weekends making holiday cookies, candies and fudge, and would climb up on the step ladder to string lights across the front of the house and in the fir tree beside it. Her favorite part had always been finding the right small cedar tree somewhere on their land and hauling it back to the house, where they decorated it with the old family ornaments. But this year she didn't put up the outside lights, and she couldn't make herself fix any goodies for the candy dishes and cookie jars. It was an effort even to go shopping for presents and food. For the first time in years the family didn't pile into the car and drive to Austin to see the Trail of Lights and the huge tree made of Christmas lights in Zilker Park. Though Julie tried to put on a good face to the world, deep down inside she wished the holiday would just disappear and leave her alone.

This year she let Riley and Cathy tramp around by themselves to find the tree. When they brought it home and set it up in the usual corner of the living room, she made hot spiced apple cider and helped them decorate it, but there was no enthusiasm in her. She did what she had to do. But all the spark, all the pleasure, were gone.

She wondered whether Tag was home for Christmas. Would he sit with his family around some elegantly decorated, perfectly symmetrical tree, set up, no doubt, by professionals? His mother would have one of those theme trees, like a Victorian one or an all-white ornaments tree like one Julie had seen in the Christmas store in Austin. The Marshalls would probably drink something like mulled wine while they contemplated the perfection of the tree, then open beautifully wrapped gifts to find things like fur coats or keys to a Jaguar or tickets to Bermuda inside.

It was a far cry from Brinkman, Texas, and a lopsided, low cedar tree covered with old ornaments. A far cry from Julie Farrell.

Of course, that was precisely why she was sitting alone like this. Why she had walked away from Tag.

Christmas was finally over, and the season crept toward New Year's Eve. Numbly, Julie went on. Someday it would get better. It had to!

One day, not long after the new year had begun, she ran into Tag at the convenience store on the highway. She was about to reach for the door when it swung open and he stepped out. He stopped, as startled as she was, and for a moment they looked at each other, saying nothing.

Finally he said, "Hello, Julie."

She gave a little nod. "Hi." It was all she could muster. She wished she had a little bit of Tag's cool. He was as handsome and calm as ever. Whatever pain he still felt over their parting, he hid it well. For some reason Julie resented that fact. She didn't notice the grim set to his mouth or the faint sadness in his eyes.

It was unbelievably awkward, standing there looking at him, unable to say anything. She cleared her throat and glanced around. His car was nowhere in sight, but she spotted one of the cattle company's pickups. No wonder she hadn't realized that Tag was there. She usually kept an eye out for his car and steered clear of wherever it was.

"How are you?" he asked. His voice was somewhat stiff, but underlying it was a note of real concern. "Have you been sick?"

"No." Julie glanced at him sharply. "Why'd you say that?"

Tag shrugged. "I don't know. You look as if you've lost weight."

She had, but she wasn't about to admit it to him. She might as well confess that she had been moping around, missing him. "I'm fine."

There was another pause, and Julie moved as though to start past him, but Tag quickly went on. "How was your Christmas?"

"Same as usual. Jill and her family came over. We had a big turkey dinner. That kind of thing. What about you? Did you go home?"

He shook his head. "No. I didn't feel like a family Christmas."

For the first time the changes in Tag's face registered on Julie. She had been too busy earlier trying not to stare at him. But now she saw the lines there that bespoke tiredness, or sadness. She saw the sparkle was missing from his intense blue eyes. A pang struck her. Was he suffering because of her?

Then she realized what a foolish question that was. What had she expected—that he would go on blithely after the woman he loved broke their engagement? He wasn't shallow. Nor was he crazy. He had loved her enough to want to marry her, and it must have been painful when she gave him back his engagement ring.

Julie sighed. She wished she could take back all the hurt she had caused. But there was no calling back the past. The worst was probably behind them. It would get easier. It *had* to get easier. Tag would recover even though he was in pain now. And her decision had been best for both of them. She and Tag simply didn't fit. They were too different. It was better to call it quits now than to get married and discover their differences later, then wind up getting divorced.

She looked away. "I—I'm sorry I hurt you. That was never something I wanted."

"But you did it. Why?"

Julie backed up. She didn't want to get into a scene right in the middle of the parking lot. One of the tellers who worked in the bank was watching them with interest while she filled the gas tank of her car. Within an hour her meeting with Tag would be all over the bank, and by the end of the day all over town. There was no method of communication in the world as fast as the Brinkman grapevine.

"Tag, please...let's not talk about this now, all right?"

"Then when can we talk? We need to discuss it. It's not fair of you to make this one-sided, irrational decision about us."

"Irrational!"

"Yes, dammit, irrational! What else would you call it when a woman tells you that she loves you but she won't marry you because your parents are different from hers?"

"There was more to it than that...."

"Was there? Then why don't you tell me what, because I didn't understand it. Then or now."

"Do we have to go through this again? I told you why it's a bad idea for us to get married."

"You didn't tell me anything I can accept."

"I can't help that. I told you the truth."

"As you see it. That's not necessarily the way it is. Why would my parents' life-style be such a problem for you?"

"Oh, Tag, don't be obtuse. It's not just your parents' life-style. It's yours, too. It's the way you were brought up. You might as well be from another planet for all we have in common. Once the passion's died down, all the cracks will start to show."

"I never intended for the passion to die down."

His face looked deadly serious. It made Julie feel weak in the knees. God, but she wanted him! Just being this close to him—hearing his voice, seeing his face—sent passion racing through her. She couldn't stop thinking about the times they had made love. The times he had kissed her. The times they had danced together, lost in a world of their own.

"And what makes you so sure," Tag continued, "that there would have be any cracks? We've gotten along fine the whole time we've known each other. Why would we suddenly change?"

"People change when they get married. Things that didn't seem so important are all of a sudden very big."

"What is it with you? Do you have a crystal ball that you can look in and see our future? How do you know what's going to happen? And how the hell are you so sure of what I'm going to do or say or feel when *I* don't have any idea?"

Tears started in her eyes. "Tag, please…" She could barely retain control of her voice. There was a quaver at the end of her words. "This is best. I just know it."

"There are times when you are absolutely infuriating." Tag sighed. "Ah, hell, don't cry. I didn't mean to make you cry." He laid a hand on her arm comfortingly.

Even through her winter jacket Julie felt the shock of his touch, and she almost jumped back from him.

"I'm sorry," he went on. "It's just that I'm so damned lonely for you. I think about you all the time. Nothing's any good anymore without you. I wish you'd come back."

Tears slid down Julie's cheeks, and she dashed them away. She couldn't go into the store now. Not in this state. She had to leave, to get away. She turned without saying anything and started walking toward her car, tears blinding her eyes. Tag ran after her and caught her by the arm, whirling her around to face him.

"Look at me. Tell the truth. Do you love me?"

Julie swallowed and looked everywhere but at his face. "I love you." Her voice was low and clogged with tears.

"Then why? Why are you doing your best to make us both miserable?"

"I tried to tell you...."

"I know. We're too different." He clenched his teeth for a moment. Then he said, his voice forcibly calm, "If you don't want to get married, that's okay. I can live with it. We can still be together. We can live together. We can date. Have an affair. Whatever you want. I just don't want to lose you entirely."

"I don't want to lose you, either! I can't bear to."

Tag made a disgusted noise. "How can you say that when you shoved me out the door?" He stopped, and his face grew thoughtful. "Wait a minute. I think I'm beginning to understand. You're scared, aren't you? All this talk about how different we are and how we could never get along in the long run—that's all it is. Just talk. The truth is you're flat out scared to marry me."

"Don't be silly."

"I'm not. I don't know why I didn't see it before. I must have been too blinded by my own anger and frustration. You're afraid of marriage. Afraid of making that commitment, of loving someone that much. That's it, isn't it?"

"No!" Julie's voice was choked. She knew that in another minute she would break down completely and cry. She whirled around to walk away, but Tag grabbed her arm again.

"Wait! Do you think I'm going to let you walk away just like that?"

"You don't have any choice!" Julie twisted her arm out of his grasp. "It's over!"

"No, it's not. Not by a long shot. There's no way I'm going to let you throw away both our lives. I love you, and I know you love me. All my life I've never had any kind of a center, any feeling of home. I've been drifting and aimless. Talented at some things, but never committed enough to stick to them. But that's changed. With you I finally found an anchor for my life. I'm committed to you like I've never been to anything else. I will not give up on you. I'm going to stay right here and I'll keep coming back until you marry me."

"I won't." Her voice trembled on the words. Tears were streaming down her face.

"Sweetheart, don't you see? There's no need to be scared. Whatever it is that frightens you, you'll have me with you to help you get through it."

"That's not always the way it works out." She swiped at her tears.

"Is this something to do with your parents? Losing them both so suddenly? Is that what you're afraid will happen again?"

"Damn it, Tag! Leave me alone! Go back to North Carolina and let me live my life!"

"There's no way I'm going back. I'm building a business I care about here. The woman I love is here. I'm afraid you're stuck with me living in Brinkman."

"You don't belong here."

"I belong wherever I make a place for myself. So do you. So does everyone. All those barriers you see, all the complications—they're in your head. They're what you make of them, and I'm not afraid to get rid of them.''

Julie whirled and walked away rapidly. More tears were pouring down her cheeks, and she barely reached the privacy of her car before a sob escaped her lips. She couldn't stand this. It was so hard seeing Tag, fighting against something she wanted desperately to do, hearing him pour out his hopes and love for her.

Life wasn't supposed to be this way! Why wasn't anything ever cut away from her life cleanly? There were always these trailing tendrils of pain hanging on, reminding her of the loss—like bleeding wounds that never quite healed. It had been that way long after her parents died. No matter how much she worked, how hard she looked after the family, how upbeat she tried to appear for her siblings' sakes, there had always been that dragging sadness inside, reminding her.

Now she felt it again for Tag. But this time it seemed even worse—this time she herself had made the wound.

Julie drove back to the feed store, brushing away the tears as they fell. She pulled into the parking lot and stopped. Turning off the engine, she leaned her forehead against the steering wheel and gave way to the sobs.

It was a long time before her crying finally quieted. She wiped away the tears with tissues, but there was no hiding her red, swollen eyes. She hated to go inside, knowing that Granddad would notice and comment on it. With a sigh she got out of the car and went in the back door of the feed store. Horace looked up when she entered and continued to watch her as she crossed the room and sat down on the stool behind the counter.

"Did we get much business while I was gone?" she asked.

He shrugged. "Some. It's been a slow afternoon." He paused. "Sure must have taken you a long time to get those drinks."

"Drinks?"

"Yeah, the ones that were on special over at Frank's."

"Oh. Yeah."

"You going to put them in the fridge?" He gestured toward the tiny refrigerator they had behind the counter, where they kept drinks, snacks and lunches.

Julie sighed. There was no getting out of this. He was definitely on the trail now. "I didn't get them."

His eyebrows went up, although he said nothing.

"Oh, all right!" she snapped. "I saw Tag at Frank's, and we had an argument. That's why I didn't get the drinks and why I took so long. There. Are you satisfied?"

He came closer and leaned against the counter. "Not really. Not when you look like you've been crying for a week."

"It wasn't anything. I just cried for a few minutes."

"That's something. I know how often you give way to crying jags."

"It's an impossible situation. I love him. And I felt bad because I've obviously hurt him."

"Not to mention yourself."

She shrugged.

"You know, honey," her grandfather went on conversationally, "I don't see what would have been so awful about ya'll getting married."

"Not you, too! It wouldn't have worked out. Eventually we would both have been miserable. We're too different."

"You mean more miserable than the two of you are now?" He shook his head. "Whew! That must be pretty powerful misery."

"Granddad, I'm serious."

"So am I. I mean, how much worse could you feel if you married him than you do right now?"

"I don't know. And I don't want to find out!" She grimaced. "Everybody acts like it would be so simple, but it's not!"

"I would never think that marriage is simple. But sometimes I wonder if the whole thing's quite as complicated as you make out."

"He told me I was scared," Julie blurted out. She hadn't intended to talk to anyone about Tag's accusations, but somehow the words had escaped her. "He said it wasn't any of the reasons I gave him. It was just because I was scared to get married. Afraid to commit myself."

"Do you think that's true?"

"I don't know! I can't help but think about what he said and wonder if he's right. What if I've been lying to myself?"

Horace gazed at her unblinkingly for a moment, his face contorted into a thoughtful frown. "There might be something to it if what he said makes you wonder that much about it. But you know, I've never seen you back away from anything because you were scared."

"Not if I realized I was scared—and I knew why I was. I can go on, even if I'm afraid, if I know what I'm getting into. But with Tag, I'm not sure of anything. Oh, Granddad, I'm so confused!"

"And unhappy. Honey, there's only one thing I've ever wanted for you, and that's for you to be happy. I hate seeing you so miserable."

"I hate *being* miserable." She sighed and propped her elbow on the counter, leaning her head against her hand. "He asked me if I was frightened because of what happened to Mom and Dad. It made me feel weird when he said that. Shaky."

Her grandfather said nothing, just waited patiently for her to continue.

"I swore I'd never feel that unhappy again." Her gaze was wistful. "I promised myself that I would take such good care of the kids that nothing would ever happen to them. They were all I had, and I couldn't stand to lose anybody again."

She looked up at her grandfather.

"It looks to me like you might have talked yourself around until an answer came out."

"You mean you think he's right."

"What do you think?"

Tears glistened in Julie's eyes. "I'm afraid maybe he is. The thought of feeling that kind of loss again terrifies me. That day when we helped you put out the fire in the front pasture, there was a moment when I thought Tag was going to get trapped and burned. I went cold all over. It terrified me."

"Wasn't that right before you broke off your engagement?" Horace asked softly.

"Yeah. Oh God." Julie's throat closed up. She ran her hand up into her hair, bending her head down. She felt like bursting into tears. The truth suddenly lay before her, and she knew with her whole being that it *was* the truth. Tag was right. It wasn't because they were different that she had split up with him. What had triggered her decision had been the fire. She had seen how easy it would be to lose Tag, and the thought of that had been more than she could bear. She had quickly shut it out of her brain, willing herself not to think about it.

But while she might cut off thought, she couldn't cut off her emotions. They knew. They understood. And she had come up with a reason to break their engagement that was easier for her to accept. "Oh, Granddad, I'm a coward! I never thought I was."

"You're not a coward. Everybody has things that are too frightening to even think about. You're human, that's all. Your problem is that you try too hard to be superhuman. To be perfect. You're going to fail every single time that way."

"I know I'm not perfect."

"Hmmph. Try telling that to somebody who'll buy it. For the past five years you've been trying to be the perfect mother and father to your brothers and sisters, as well as the perfect businesswoman, the perfect grandchild. Sometimes I think you hope you can stave off all bad things just by being perfect."

Julie began to cry again. "I'm sorry. I'm such an emotional idiot these day."

"There's nothing wrong with that. It's way past time you were. Honey, you've been strong for everybody for a long time. Everyone else got a chance to be weak, including me, but not you. I think it's time you gave in to it.''

"I wish Mom and Dad were here to tell me what to do," Julie whispered. "I still miss them."

"So do I. I don't think that's something that ever quite goes away."

She straightened, pushing back her hair from her face. "So." She cleared her throat and struggled to assume a cool, reasonable attitude. "I broke off with Tag because I'm scared. Knowing that doesn't make me any less afraid. I don't want to marry him and lose him!''

"Looks to me like you're losing him anyway."

"Yes, but...surely it doesn't hurt as much this way. And I don't have to spend my life wondering if it will happen."

"Maybe that's true. But you'll spend it wondering whether you did the right thing. Wondering if you missed out on the best thing in life, and all for nothing. What if you don't lose him? You can't assume you will. The odds are he won't die for a long, long time. And what makes you think that, loving you like he does, he'll leave you? You want to put your whole future on the line on the off chance that you might lose him?''

Julie stared at him, at a loss for words.

"Tell me this, then. Do you think that if your Mom and Dad had known when they were going to die they would have said, 'Well, let's not have any kids because we'll lose them in twenty years.'? Or would you have preferred, since they had to die, that you had never known them at all?"

"Oh, no! I'm grateful for having had them for nineteen years. I wouldn't have given them up."

"Then why do you want to give up Tag because you might lose him someday?"

Julie looked away, unable to answer him. Her emotions churned inside her, confused and disturbed. "I— I have to get away. I have to think. Would you lock up the store tonight?"

"Sure."

"Thanks." She gave him a distracted smile and grabbed her purse. She walked out of the store, pausing in the doorway to turn back to him. "You're a really smart guy. Did you know that?"

"The old country philosopher, that's me," Horace joked.

Julie got into her car and began to drive, aimlessly at first, until she realized that she had turned unconsciously onto the road to the cemetery. Then she knew where she wanted to go, had to go, and she slowed down and turned in at the cemetery's black wrought iron gates. She drove slowly to the rear of the cemetery and stopped. She got out of the car and headed down the walk to a crosspath. There, on the corner, at the edge of generations of Farrells, lay the double headstone and the graves of her parents.

Automatically Julie reached down and plucked the few errant weeds that had taken root around the plot. She ran her hand along the top of the stone, then sat down on the flat marble border around the plot and pulled her knees up, wrapping her arms around them. She rested her chin on her knees and sat gazing at the tombstone. Loving Wife, Anna. Loving Husband,

John. Her mother had been just shy of her fortieth birthday when she had been killed.

It seemed an awfully short time to have lived. But her mother had often commented on how full her life was. "Johnny promised me that life would never be dull with him," she was fond of saying, grinning and casting her husband a teasing look. "And he was sure right about that." She had borne five children and loved them dearly. Somehow she had treated them in such a way that each child had been convinced that he or she was their mother's favorite. And, in a way, Julie guessed that they had all been right. Julie had been her oldest, her "right hand." Cathy had been her youngest, her "shining glory." Riley was his mother's "dreamer," and she had sat many times listening with starry eyes to the stories he spun. Jill had been her "beauty," her "flirt," and Lyle had been her "joker," the personality. Each of them had been special to her. Would she have given up a single one of them, knowing that she would have to leave them young?

Not a chance. Julie knew the answer without having to think about it. Even if someone could have traded her mother a long life without family for her brief one with them, Anna would never have accepted the offer. She had loved her husband, her children and every minute of her life.

Nor would her father have made that trade. People used to joke that he worshipped the ground Anna walked on and thought his kids were the greatest in the world. She remembered him at Lyle's Pony League football games, cheering as if it were the Super Bowl. Or working the concession stand at the football games for the parent group when she was in high school, laughing and joking with the kids, waving at her across the way. She remembered, too, chasing fireflies through the summer dusk with her brothers and sisters while Mom and Dad sat cuddled together on the porch swing, as close as a couple of teenagers, talking and giggling together.

The two of them had loved each other so much that it was almost a joke around town. When their car had crashed, many people had said comfortingly, "Well, at least they went together. That's the way they would have liked it." Julie was sure that was true.

Neither one of them would have hesitated to take a chance on love.

Julie turned her face down, resting her forehead on the bony plateau of her knees. Hot tears stung her eyes. Could there be anything more wonderful than experiencing love like that? Even if by chance it ended after a short while, wouldn't it have been worth it? She cried, the drops splashing down onto her denim-clad legs, cried in heartrending sobs that she hadn't let loose since the dorm mother had told her about the accident.

After a while she raised her head. The world was blurry from the tears in her eyes, and her head ached. She was sure her face looked blotched and swollen.

But none of that mattered. There was a kind of peace inside her now. And more than that, there was an excitement, a joy. How could she have been so stupid? So scared? There wasn't anything in the world that could compare to the kind of love she felt for Tag. She would never be happy without him. And nothing could ever make up for not having him. There wasn't enough content and quiet and peace in the world to make up for Tag's absence.

Julie jumped to her feet and walked back to her car, dusting off the seat of her pants. She got in and drove straight through town to the road leading up to the B & K Cattle Company. She turned the radio up loud and sang as she drove, feeling suddenly as light and buoyant as a balloon.

She saw the changes as soon as she reached the ranch. On the right-hand side of the driveway, across from the cattle pens and barn, a new horse barn was going up. Already there were white-painted pipe fences slicing the land into large rectangular paddocks. Tag had obviously been serious when he said he planned to stay here and add a horse operation to the ranch.

Julie pulled to a stop in front of the main house and walked up to the door. She knocked and waited, but there was no answer. Disappointment stabbed her. She turned to go back to the car.

Then she saw him. Tag was walking out of the door of the nearby guest house that Mike had long ago turned into an office. He was talking to another man, who had a pad and pencil and was nodding vigorously. Tag glanced toward the house and saw her. He stopped. The other man walked on a few steps, then turned in confusion. Tag looked steadily at Julie for a moment, then said something to the man and started walking away from him, straight toward Julie. The other man shrugged and started off toward the horse barn. Tag's strides grew longer and quicker with each passing second, until he was almost running.

He stopped a few feet away and they gazed at each other. Julie's throat dried up. Now that the moment was here, she could think of nothing to say.

Finally, inconsequentially, she began, "You look different from when you came here."

Gone was the immaculate gentleman who had arrived in the silk Italian suit. He wore work-scarred boots, faded jeans, a flannel shirt and a denim jacket to keep out the chill. His hair was longer and shaggier. He obviously hadn't been to Austin in a while to get it cut.

"I am different from when I came here," he replied.

"I guess that's true." She took a deep breath. "I came to tell you that you were right."

He straightened a little, and something flared in his eyes, then was quickly masked. "About what?"

"About me. I *was* afraid." She felt a flush rising in her cheeks. How did you go about taking back a refusal to marry someone? "I—I don't know how to say this."

"You don't have to." He tucked his fingers into one of the pockets of his jeans and pulled out her engagement ring. He held it out in the palm of his hand. "Just take it back."

With trembling fingers she reached out and took the ring from his hand. She slid it onto her finger and looked up at him. "I love you, Tag. I'm sorry. I'm sorry for all the pain I caused you."

He made a negating gesture and came to her, his arms encircling her and pulling her to him. They kissed, long and deeply.

"God, I'm glad you came back," he told her. "I missed you like hell."

"Me too."

"I love you. I'm never letting you go again." He nuzzled her hair. "I have so many things I've been storing up to tell you. I want to show you everything—the new buildings, the paddocks..."

"I want to see them."

He kissed her again, hard. "I'll take you." He looked down at her, his arms loosely holding her. Then he grinned devilishly. "But those'll have to wait. There are other, more important things, that come first."

Julie shrieked with surprise as he suddenly lifted her high off the ground. He flung her onto his shoulder and started for the house at a lope. Their laughter mingled and floated out behind them through the air.

And Julie knew that whatever the future brought, their love would make it all worthwhile.

*   *   *   *   *

WRITTEN IN THE STARS

A Lasting Love

The passionate Cancer man is destined for love this July in Val Whisenand's FOR ETERNITY, the latest in our compelling WRITTEN IN THE STARS series.

Sexy Adam Gaines couldn't explain the eerie sense of familiarity that arose each time his eyes met Kate Faraday's. But Mexico's steamy jungles were giving the star-crossed lovers another chance to make their love last for all eternity....

FOR ETERNITY by Val Whisenand is coming this July from Silhouette Romance. It's WRITTEN IN THE STARS!

Silhouette Special Edition

presents

SONNY'S GIRLS

by Emilie Richards, Celeste Hamilton and Erica Spindler

They had been Sonny's girls, irresistibly drawn to the charismatic high school football hero. Ten years later, none could forget the night that changed their lives forever.

In July—
ALL THOSE YEARS AGO by Emilie Richards (SSE #684)
Meredith Robbins had left town in shame. Could she ever banish the past and reach for love again?

In August—
DON'T LOOK BACK by Celeste Hamilton (SSE #690)
Cyndi Saint was Sonny's steady. Ten years later, she remembered only his hurtful parting words....

In September—
LONGER THAN... by Erica Spindler (SSE #696)
Bubbly Jennifer Joyce was everybody's friend. But nobody knew the secret longings she felt for bad boy Ryder Hayes....

SSESG-1

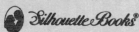

You'll flip . . . your pages won't!
Read paperbacks *hands-free* with

Book Mate • I

The perfect "mate" for all your romance paperbacks

Traveling • Vacationing • At Work • In Bed • Studying • Cooking • Eating

Perfect size for all standard paperbacks, this wonderful invention makes reading a pure pleasure! Ingenious design holds paperback books OPEN and FLAT so even wind can't ruffle pages— leaves your hands free to do other things. Reinforced, wipe-clean vinyl-covered holder flexes to let you turn pages without undoing the strap...supports paperbacks so well, they have the strength of hardcovers!

Pages turn WITHOUT opening the strap

SEE-THROUGH STRAP

Reinforced back stays flat

Built in bookmark

BOOK MARK

BACK COVER HOLDING STRIP

10˝ x 7¼˝ . opened.
Snaps closed for easy carrying. too

Available now. Send your name, address, and zip code, along with a check or money order for just $5.95 + .75¢ for delivery (for a total of $6.70) payable to Reader Service to:

Reader Service
Bookmate Offer
3010 Walden Avenue
P.O. Box 1396
Buffalo, N.Y. 14269-1396

Offer not available in Canada
*New York residents add appropriate sales tax.

BM-GR

SILHOUETTE·INTIMATE·MOMENTS®

IT'S TIME TO MEET
THE MARSHALLS!

In 1986, bestselling author Kristin James wrote A VERY SPECIAL FAVOR for the Silhouette Intimate Moments line. Hero Adam Marshall quickly became a reader favorite, and ever since then, readers have been asking for the stories of his two brothers, Tag and James. At last your prayers have been answered!

In June, look for Tag's story, SALT OF THE EARTH (IM #385). Then skip a month and look for THE LETTER OF THE LAW (IM #393— August), starring James Marshall. And, as our very special favor to you, we'll be reprinting A VERY SPECIAL FAVOR this September. Look for it in special displays wherever you buy books.

MARSH-1

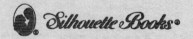

Silhouette Books®